"What hap

Justin kept his ey[...] happened? He'd discovered the man he disliked most in the world had married the most beautiful woman he'd ever seen and they were having a baby together.

"That's her," Justin said to the other paramedic. "That's the woman I met in the coffee shop. The one I was telling you about earlier."

"Wow. Is that the reason you froze? Because this lady smiled at you in a coffee shop?"

"Can't we talk about this later? How's she doing?" Justin asked.

"She's stable," Matt said. "I don't know about the baby."

An ache rushed through Justin. Kirkpatrick or not, he didn't want this woman to lose her baby. No matter what Tommy had done to him and his family.

"So when did Tommy move back to Glendale?" Justin said.

"Man, you really don't know, do you?"

"Know what?" Justin glanced at his friend in the rearview mirror.

"Tommy Kirkpatrick is dead."

Books by Kit Wilkinson

Love Inspired

Mom in the Making

Love Inspired Suspense

Protector's Honor
Sabotage

KIT WILKINSON

is a former Ph.D. student who once wrote discussions on the medieval feminine voice. She now prefers weaving stories of romance and redemption. Her first inspirational manuscript won the prestigious RWA Golden Heart and her second has been nominated for the RT Reviewer's Choice Awards. You can visit with Kit at www.kitwilkinson.com or write to her at write@kitwilkinson.com.

Mom in the Making

Kit Wilkinson

Love Inspired

Recycling programs
for this product may
not exist in your area.

 LOVE INSPIRED BOOKS

ISBN-13: 978-0-373-87684-6

MOM IN THE MAKING

Copyright © 2011 by Kit Wilkinson

www.LoveInspiredBooks.com

Printed in U.S.A.

"Look," said Naomi, "your sister-in-law is going back to her people and her gods. Go back with her."

But Ruth replied, "Don't urge me to leave you or to turn back from you. Where you go I will go, and where you stay I will stay. Your people will be my people and your God my God."
—*Ruth* 1:15–16

To my own mother-in-law, Pamela Charlotte,
who has always been my good friend

and

To my daughter, Charlotte Taylor,
may your love for the Lord continue to grow as you do

Chapter One

"Wait a minute, miss. That's mine." Wasn't that *his* coffee? Justin Winters stood wide-eyed as a tall blonde slipped away from the pick-up counter with a steaming cup of fresh coffee. He double-checked the number on his ticket. Thirty-two. Yep, that *was* his coffee. And he wanted it. Badly. The strong aroma of fresh Colombian had tantalized his senses long enough. "Hel-lo-o. Excuse me, ma'am. That's my order."

Oblivious to his calls, she continued off with the coffee in her hands. Justin hurried after her, ducking his head a few times to avoid the fancy light fixtures that hung too low for anyone over six-two, meaning they hit him right in the nose. He tapped her shoulder. She turned. Long, golden curls flipped and bounced over the collar of her jacket then settled around her soft face. And, oh, what a face!

Justin froze, forgetting all about the cup of coffee he'd wanted so desperately. In fact, the beautiful woman could keep the coffee. Coffee was nothing. Not when compared to peachy lips stretching into a sweet smile, a perfect dimple on the left cheek and a brilliant set of clear, azure eyes. Those things had coffee beat hands down.

She pulled a pair of earbuds away from her head and

shoved them into an oversize shoulder bag. She glanced up at him, blue eyes gleaming. "Sorry. Did I forget something?"

No. But he had. He'd forgotten how to speak. The Afghan war zone hadn't provided a lot of views like the one in front of him and it had rendered him senseless, turning him into a gawking, gaping Neanderthal. Mouth open, arms dangling, the whole bit.

"Did you need something?" she asked.

"I did." Justin jerked a smile over his face, stretched his torso long and tall, and reached up to rub a hand through his buzz cut. Instead of his hair, his fingers whacked one of the light fixtures, sending it into orbit around his head. So much for a good first impression. *Smooth move, Winters.*

He steadied the light. The woman's crystal blue eyes opened wide with amusement. Justin cleared his throat, hoping to swallow down his own embarrassment. He'd never been too suave around the women, but this was a rather rough start even for him. He *had* stopped her for a reason, right? His eyes made a quick scan of the surroundings.

"Coffee," he said, as if locating a set of misplaced keys. "You—you took my coffee."

Her smile grew wider and Justin thought he might go weak in the knees.

"Oh, dear," she said. "I guess my music was too loud. I heard the wrong number. Sorry. Here."

She handed him the drink and flowed gracefully back to the counter, the loose fabric of her dress and jacket billowing behind her. A soft, clean scent way more tantalizing than ground coffee beans swirled around him as she moved away, and then again as she crossed back in front of him with a different cup in her hands. Justin drank in all of her—her classic bone structure, her peachy colored cheeks and her perky nose. She was a beauty with a face he'd never forget. It was also one he'd never seen before, which, in a town as small as Glendale, Tennessee, could only mean one thing— she was new.

"Glad you caught me," she said, glancing over her shoulder as she passed back by him still standing there like a statue cemented to the floor. "I don't even drink coffee. Herbal tea."

She floated away again. This time to the fixings table where she dumped two or three packets of raw sugar into her cup and proceeded to stir rapidly with a wooden stick.

Justin followed her to the table as if a string were attached between them. He poured a generous portion of half and half into his coffee, even though he preferred it black, and struggled to put a thought together.

He was as nervous as if he was waiting for his final test into the 101st Army Airborne. Even his palms were sweating, and it wasn't because of the hot coffee in his hands. And why? He certainly wasn't in the market for romance. Far from it. He was already married to his work. And that's the way he liked it. So why was he reacting so strongly to this woman?

He hardly knew, but he couldn't seem to stop himself. He grabbed a napkin from the counter and wiped his moist hands, pretending something sticky had spread on his fingers. She looked up at him again and smiled. His heart pounded against his ribs.

"Glendale Emergency Medical Team." She squinted to read the crest on his shirt as she leaned across the counter to throw away her tea bags. "You're a paramedic? That must be interesting work. How long have you done that?"

"W-well—" His voice cracked. He paused and swallowed hard. "Actually, it's my first day on the team here in Glendale. I just came home from active duty." He decided to leave out the part that he'd been *sent* home to recover from Post Traumatic Stress.

"What branch of service?"

"Army."

"Really? Like a Ranger or Delta Force?"

He blushed a little. "More like the 101st Airborne."

"Wow. So you're a pilot and a medic?"

"Sort of."

"Sort of?" She lifted an eyebrow, grinning at his vague answers, but seemed uninterested in pushing her questions. He was glad. He wasn't in the mood for explaining that he was neither of those things but still more than qualified to wear the medic uniform.

"Hmm. That's interesting," she continued. "Never heard of that but it sure makes being a sixth-grade teacher sound really boring."

"No way. A middle-school teacher? Now *that* is a dangerous job."

She smiled and took a sip of tea. "Sometimes it can be."

Justin gulped his coffee, forgetting both that it was hot and that it had cream in it. He could only imagine the face he'd made. She didn't seem to notice.

"So you're from Glendale?"

"Born and bred." He nodded. "But you're not?"

"Nope. Atlanta. Been here a few months. But I just got a job today. So, who knows, maybe I'll stay."

"Congratulations." So she *was* new to town. And now that he thought about it, people only moved to Glendale for two reasons—either to attend the university or to marry someone who already lived here. Suddenly, he felt silly. She was married. Of course. She had to be. He glanced down at her ring finger. Not that he cared or anything. He didn't. He was home to heal his mind. Not to date. But he could be curious, right? No harm in that?

Her left hand hugged the cup of tea. No rings. It was bare.

Justin smiled wider. "It's not easy to find work these days. That's great."

"I know. I was very fortunate. Although it is temporary and certainly not as exciting as being a medic and a pilot."

"Yeah, I don't know how exciting being a medic in Glendale is going to be. In fact, I'm on duty right now and you see that I'm here at the coffee shop. I don't think we get many calls." He paused and took a sip of coffee, bracing himself for the unwelcomed taste of cream. "So you must be either teaching at Glendale or Lakeview. Those were the only two middle schools in the county when I was growing up, and I don't think that's changed."

"Lakeview. I'll be filling in for Mrs. Fox while she's on maternity leave."

"Then you'll meet my little sister. She's a teacher there, too." Justin lifted a brow, thinking that might be convenient. "Her name is Katie Winters. Look her up when you start."

She nodded sweetly, her golden waves following the soft motion of her head. A little blush rose to her cheeks.

Man. She sure was pretty. Justin wanted to ask her her name and find out a little more about her. He wanted to keep talking to her, and not just because she was beautiful. Although she *was* beautiful. There was something else there, too. Some feeling she'd awakened inside him. Feelings long buried through years of living in a combat zone and focusing single-mindedly on his work. If only he had time in his life to explore such feelings now. But he did not.

Justin was home for one thing and one thing only. To heal his mind so that he could get back to the army and do his job. He was the one flight surgeon for a very large airborne division. The pilots needed him and his expertise. They did not need a doctor with his head in a fog over women or traumatic combat experiences. But Justin had a feeling this wasn't just any woman. This was the kind of woman who made him think of family and relationships and all those things he'd put on hold to pursue his work in the medical field.

Becky Rhodes Kirkpatrick took a step back from the tall, dark and extremely hunky medic. The conversation had become a little awkward. The man was probably harmless enough, but she had definitely caught him glancing at her ring finger. Next, he'd be telling her his name and asking her out for coffee….

"I'm Justin," he said, before she'd completely turned away. "Justin Winters."

Becky pressed her lips together in hesitation. Should she tell him the truth? Tell him she was a widow and that she was five months pregnant?

Ha. No. Talk about awkward.

Anyway, it was refreshing to meet someone who didn't already know who she was and her whole tragic story. In the past few weeks, sympathies had grown tiresome. As had the look of shock on people's faces when she told them she was expecting. And yet, somehow this innocent conversation had started to feel a bit untruthful. Being tall and naturally thin, she hardly looked pregnant. On the other hand, saying *"I'm a pregnant widow"* didn't exactly flow into the conversation.

"I'm Becky," she answered.

He gave her hand a firm but gentle shake. "Nice to meet you, Becky."

She caught the flecks of gold sparkling in his chocolate eyes. They glowed with intensity and interest. Yeah. Too much interest. Becky lowered her head. Good grief. Was she blushing? Ugh. Now he would think she was flirting. And she could not possibly be flirting. The heat in her cheeks was probably another influx of pregnancy hormones. In any case, it was time to go. And quickly. "Nice to meet you, too. I'll be sure to look your sister up when I start teaching next week."

The paramedic nodded and waved a hand through the air as Becky walked out of the shop. She smiled. In fact, she was smiling so hard her jaw ached. And it felt good. It had been far too long. Tommy would not have been pleased with all her crying and mourning and depression. He would have reminded her that God was in control and that she was in His will. He would have wanted her to get out and enjoy herself and get on with life. He would have wanted her to smile. Like she was doing now.

And Glendale was such a beautiful town. She'd had no idea. Tommy had called his hometown—a sprawling little establishment centered around a large lake on the Tennessee plateau—a country paradise, a place where it was easy to see the hand of the Lord everywhere you looked. Becky couldn't have agreed more. She took in a deep breath, wondering what Tommy would have thought about her encounter with the medic. Would he mind that she'd enjoyed a conversation with another man? No. She let out a bittersweet giggle. He would have put his arm around her and said he'd picked the prettiest girl in the South and everyone else would just have to deal with it. How she missed his arms around her shoulders, how she hated being alone, how she feared she would always be alone….

Becky walked on to her car. A flood of images and sounds from the past filled her mind.

Please. Promise me…

Sometimes she could still hear Tommy's voice, so weak from the cancer and the first and only chemo treatment, which had killed him within a few hours. Becky shook her head and climbed into her car. Her smile faded, replaced with the emotionless front she'd learned to display in place of tears when she thought of how alone she was now that Tommy was gone.

At times, she wanted to shut out the thoughts and memories of Tommy. At other times, like at this moment, it bothered her that the true timbre of his voice had begun to fade from her mind...the particular gray of his eyes, his unique swagger as he crossed a room, the way his hair flopped over his forehead in one big curl. She didn't want to forget these things. The two of them had had such little time together. Still, it didn't seem right she could forget everything so quickly. And yet, the image of him had already begun to lose color in her mind. Maybe if she'd paid more attention. Noted the exact curve of his nose and the placement of the freckles on his cheeks. But she'd never thought of the possibility of waking up to a world where there was no Tommy. Even though she'd done it for nearly five months now.

Stay with her. Tell my mother about Christ. I'm not going to get the chance...

It hadn't been the only reason Becky had moved in with her mother-in-law, but Tommy's words had been a driving force. Of course, she would have promised him anything as he lay there dying of leukemia.

And so, the last five months had been a blur. She'd made decisions without really thinking—she'd sold their home and Tommy's car; found another family to take in their dog; quit her teaching job. All because of her promise.

A promise she'd never dreamed would be so difficult to honor. Living with Aggie should have been like living with family, but it wasn't. The stern, disapproving woman was nothing like the mother Becky had lost years ago. And giving up the home and the life she and Tommy had shared just made those happy memories seem even further away. Perhaps Tommy hadn't thought about the hardships his request would cause. And it didn't matter, Becky was determined to keep her word. No matter how difficult. No matter how tired she felt. And boy, did she feel tired at that moment.

Perhaps she'd overdone things that morning—getting the job after taking a long walk around the lake. Becky started her car. As the engine revved, so did the pain in her head. Her vision blurred and a strange lifting sensation took her by surprise.

She grabbed hold of her belly as the intense pain traveled from her right side to the left, squeezing the air from her lungs and causing her to bend at the waist. Nausea waved over her, leaving her exhausted and lifeless. She hoped nothing was wrong. That she was just tired. But was it ever good to have pain during a pregnancy? She closed her eyes tight, not allowing her mind to go there. She couldn't bear another loss. That very thought filled her with such a crippling fear that she often, strangely, found herself unwilling to think of the dear, precious life inside her. Still, as soon as she got home, she would call the doctor and schedule a checkup.

Slowly, the cramp released and she recovered her breath. She drove out of the coffee-shop parking lot and headed for home. Well, not home exactly. It was Greyfield. Aggie's home. Tommy's home. Not her home.

She sighed, disappointed with her unkind thoughts. She needed to be more appreciative of her mother-in-law. It couldn't be easy for the woman to open her home to a daughter-in-law she hardly knew and had never approved of. The arrangement was awkward at best, but it did, in theory, make sense. Especially as Becky had no family of her own. Tommy had been her family. And Tommy had wanted her to stay with Aggie, at least until the baby was born. It was reasonable and manageable. And yes, very difficult.

Within fifteen minutes, Becky drove onto the grounds of Greyfield, the Kirkpatricks' little piece of Glendale, wondering how she was going to tell Aggie about the job at the middle school. To say her mother-in-law would be displeased with the idea would be like saying the sun was a little warm.

She parked her mini in the garage bay that Aggie had cleared for her stay, then crossed through the pristine rose gardens toward the large limestone house—a house as cold-looking on the outside as it felt on the inside. How alone Tommy must have felt growing up in such a place. A home should be warm, Becky thought. A place filled with pictures and memories of good times together. Not one filled with marble carvings and ironworks that had no significance or meaning to anyone except their momentary value. She would never have traded one inch of her life in the tiny Atlanta apartment with her own mother for all fifty acres of Greyfield.

Becky let herself into the front of the home, noticing the three cars parked under the carport. Bridge day. Aggie had company. This would be good. She would be distracted. Becky could slip off to her own room, call the doctor's office and talk to Aggie about the teaching job later. Like at dinner.

Dinner. Becky checked her watch. Uh-oh. Lunch. She'd missed lunch, since as usual she hadn't felt hungry. She hadn't even thought of it. Not that it mattered, except that Aggie was adamant about keeping a schedule. Something else Becky would like to discuss with her mother-in-law. At some point. Not today, when she was feeling so drained.

Becky stepped into the marble foyer and removed the long jacket that matched her dress. Aggie and her friends chatted in a nearby room until she walked by and they all fell silent.

Aggie cleared her throat. "You missed lunch. I left your soup and salad on the kitchen counter."

"Thank you." Becky turned into the den where Aggie, Mrs. Burns, Mrs. Kelly and Mrs. Fitzwilliams were gathered around the card table, each with a soda in front of them and a pair of reading glasses hanging around their necks. "Hello, ladies," she called to them. "I forgot it was bridge day. Sorry to interrupt."

"Nonsense, girl," said Mrs. Kelly. "It's good to see you. You add some life to this old house. How are you feeling? You look wonderful. Still can't tell you are pregnant. Look at that girl. Just as thin as a lake reed."

"I'm feeling well, thank you." No reason to complain about how tired she really was.

Aggie's friends waved and returned her smile. Embarrassment filled her cheeks with heat. Aggie never greeted her that warmly and certainly not with any compliments.

Aggie did not smile at all. In fact, she looked quite out of spirits even for Aggie. Her steely gaze zeroed in on Becky. She put her cards facedown on the table and folded her arms across her chest, releasing a long drawn-out sigh. "So, Rebecca, when were you going to tell me about your new job?"

Becky froze in the doorway of the den. How could Aggie already know about the teaching position? She'd just gotten the job. It had been little over an hour ago.

"The school called asking for you a few minutes ago. Something about your schedule. I hardly knew what to say. I was in complete shock. You know how I feel about working women. If you needed money, you should have asked me." She looked away with disgust.

"Becky," Mrs. Kelly said. "You found a job? That's wonderful. Then you'll be staying with us in Glendale. That will make Aggie very happy, won't it, Aggie?"

Aggie looked less than enthusiastic. Becky wondered what could she say to her to make her understand she needed to start a new life. Or could she? Sometimes it seemed their living together wasn't going to work out after all. Being treated like a high school kid all of the time had become unbearable. Something was going to have to change if she was going to stay there for four more months.

But if she left… The concern of moving, finding a place to live, a full-time job and money pressed in Becky's already fatigued mind, making her feel dizzy. The sharp pain grabbed hold of her core again. Then nausea. She had definitely overdone it today. If only she could go lie down. Rest. Have this conversation later. Or never.

Not wanting the others to sense her struggles, Becky fixed a pleasant expression on her face and exhaled through the cramp, hoping some steady breathing would ward off the pain.

She took another step into the large den, still thinking of the dispute with Aggie. What could she say to her? Something about the job. Something to win her over. Something to make the woman like her. This was not how she had wanted to start the conversation.

"Oh, ladies, it was all a complete surprise." She tried to hide the breathiness of her speech. "I hadn't planned to get a job at all. I just stopped by the school to ask about their substituting needs and it turns out they had a temporary position they needed to fill right now. It happens to be the subject and grade level that I teach. I've really missed working. I thought it would help the time pass until the baby is born. I didn't mean to hide anything, Aggie. Honestly, I went over to the school on a whim. I had no idea they would actually have a need."

"We'll discuss this later." Aggie pushed back her short gray hair.

Yes, we will, thought Becky, fighting the anger building up in her. How out of control everything felt.

Lord, help me love this woman. Help me show her who You are. Help me keep my promise.

"Oh, Aggie," said Mrs. Burns, under her breath. "For crying out loud, she's a grown woman. If she wants to work, let her work. Gracious. We're not living in the Dark Ages anymore. And you can hardly expect her to hang around here with us old biddies all day long."

Becky moved forward again, trying to gauge Aggie's re-action to her friend's comments, but as she turned, another shock of pain came to her belly—this time like someone had sucker-punched her in the gut. She folded over at the waist, stumbling and grabbing her midsection. The women around the bridge table gasped.

"Becky, dear?" said Mrs. Kelly. "You look ill."

She tried to hide the pain from her face, but it was difficult enough just trying to stay upright. Something was wrong. Something was terribly wrong. She'd had a cramp or two in the past week but nothing like this. This was different. And it was powerful and that scared her to death. *Lord, please not my baby, too.*

Becky steadied herself, holding on to the back of the couch, but the room continued to spin around her. The little bit of tea in her stomach came up and out.

"Aggie, call the doctor. Something's wrong," one of the women said. Becky could no longer distinguish the voices.

A chair backed away from the bridge table and screeched across the floor. Someone approached her at the couch. She couldn't see who it was. Her vision still blurred and the cramps and nausea were increasing.

I'm fine, she wanted to say but the words died on her tongue as her legs started to give way.

Frail, tender hands reached out to support her. Becky doubted they could stop her fall. She didn't want to go down but there was no avoiding it. She'd never felt so heavy in her life. Heavy. Dizzy. Ill.

She tumbled to the floor. The blurry world around her spotted into whiteness and the cold, tiled floor touched her cheek.

Then everything went black.

Chapter Two

Justin Winters sounded the ambulance siren.

"2250 Winding Oaks Drive." Matt Richardson, his medic partner, called out the address as it printed across the small computer screen. "I think that's near the Kirkpatricks' place."

Justin's cheek twitched. "That *is* the Kirkpatricks' place."

"Oh, that's right. You used to know them." Matt nodded, his eyes wide.

Of course Matt remembered the nefarious connection between the two families, Justin thought. Everyone in Glendale did. Not that anyone knew exactly what had happened—the story was skewed by time and tellers—but some fraction of it was still there. The notion that something had happened between the Winters family and the Kirkpatrick family, something so bad that neither family spoke to, of, or about the other.

Pulse rising, Justin turned the emergency van around and started driving toward the Kirkpatricks' home, Greyfield, a place he hadn't been to in years.

This is nothing. After facing insurgents in Iraq and Afghanistan, this will be nothing.

He tried to relax. Tried to go back to the peaceful frame

of mind he'd enjoyed that morning. The way he'd felt for those few minutes in the coffee shop with the beautiful middle-school teacher, Becky. But hearing the name Kirkpatrick brought bile to his throat. As they drove across town to where he'd spent every summer of his childhood before everything had gone wrong, his teeth clenched tight together and his hands choked around the steering wheel. How could his first call in Glendale be to Greyfield? Unbelievable.

Forcing his fingers to release their strong grip on the wheel, Justin was determined to focus on medicine. He was home to get his mind straight. Control his fears and other emotions so that he could go back to helping pilots. He couldn't lose sight of that at the mere mention of old trouble.

"What's the situation?" he asked Matt.

"I didn't get much. Someone passed out, I think," Matt explained.

"The pool boy, maybe?" Justin mumbled under his breath, unable to disguise his disdain.

"A female," Matt said.

Justin shook his head. "Let's pray it's not Mrs. Kirkpatrick. Even if we did everything perfectly, she'd be likely to sue us for malpractice as soon as she felt better."

"Whoa." Matt looked at him with eyebrows raised. "You okay going on this call? You seem a little tense."

"Yeah, more like a little bitter."

"A little." Matt held up his hand, a finger and thumb indicating a small amount.

"Sorry. Not too excited about going to Greyfield. But no worries. I'll be fine. I will handle it." He hoped.

Matt nodded. "I'm not a huge Kirkpatrick fan, either. But I guess I feel a little sorry for them right now...you know since they just lost a family member."

"What?" Justin asked, turning into the Kirkpatricks' long driveway. "One of the Kirkpatricks passed away?"

"Yes. You didn't know? It was just a few months ago."

Justin frowned. No, he didn't. This was the first he'd heard of any death since he'd come back home. Perhaps his family had forgotten to mention it. But since when did his family forget to pass on the town news?

He pulled up alongside three luxury sedans, unfortunately blocking the best way into the home. He threw the vehicle into Park and started out of the van, catching sight of a man out front—the gardener, from the looks of him—awaiting their approach. "You get the supply bag and the oxygen. I'll go in and start assessment."

Matt nodded respectfully. Justin hoped Matt didn't mind taking orders, but Justin was, after all, the one with the medical degree, clearly the more experienced of the two. Then again, he was also the one who'd been sent home to recover from panic attacks. Justin shook the thought away. There was no room for doubts in the field of medicine. No time for mistakes or hesitations. Or unresolved anger, for that matter.

He followed the gardener to the front door. The man nervously recounting in Spanish to him what he knew of the incident. Justin understood very little, although the word *bambino* he heard clearly as the man repeated it several times. So it was a child who'd passed out? The flash image of an injured Afghan child popped forth from the recesses of his brain. Someone he'd treated? Or was it his imagination again? The fact that he didn't know was upsetting.

They entered the home. A group of anxious looking senior women stood in the foyer, stepping aside as he moved in. He easily recognized Mrs. Kirkpatrick among them, hands on hips, and a scowl on her face. She did not look pleased to see him. He wished he could tell her the feeling was mutual. But there was no time for that. He had a job to do.

The gardener led him through the foyer into the den and around a large couch. Justin followed him, stopping short when he saw not a *bambino* but a grown woman lying motionless across the hard, tiled floor. A woman he knew. His heart skipped a beat as he recognized the soft curls of flaxen hair. There was no mistaking—it was Becky, the beautiful lady from the coffee shop. What was *she* doing here? At the Kirkpatricks' home? His stomach quivered. His hands began to tremble.

One of the older women kneeled over her body, but rose and backed away as he approached, revealing on the floor around her a pool of blood.

No. No blood. Please, Lord. Not blood.

Justin blinked hard at a circle of red around her. He took a step back and tried to focus but panic had already edged around him, swallowed him up and taken him away.

Greyfield, Becky, Mrs. Kirkpatrick—they all dissolved from his awareness. In their place, Justin found himself scrambling through the Afghan scrub. Five minutes ago, he'd touched down in a minefield. The tail of their plane had been blown to pieces. He'd carried the pilot out of the small craft just before the entire thing had caught fire and blown sky high.

Blood was on his hands, his face, his clothes. Lieutenant Gentry was limp in his arms, unconscious but not dead. Not yet. He'd been shot in the stomach. Justin had to find the rebel camp. And fast.

But he had no radio, no night-vision wear. He didn't even have a compass. He calculated his time and direction as best he could by the stars. Moving slowly under the weight of Gentry's limp body. The walk should have taken only thirty minutes. But more time than that had passed since the explosion. He must have been moving in circles. Or so it seemed.

Blood. More blood. More of Gentry's blood.

He could feel the warm, sticky flow over his hands again. Gentry's wound had reopened despite the makeshift bandage. Justin dropped to his knees, lowered the lieutenant to the earth and quickly set to work ripping his own shirt into strips to tie around the young pilot.

A tight grip took hold of his shoulder. Justin looked up. A pair of black eyes glared down into his. *Stay right there. Don't move.* The Farsi words broke through the silence of the night.

"You okay?"

A quiver spread through Justin's body. Then a hard shiver. He blinked hard. It was light. Not dark. The ground below him a cold, tiled floor. At his shoulder was Matt—Matt Richardson, the paramedic.

A burst of air released from Justin's lungs. His eyes scanned the perimeter. Living room. Kirkpatrick. Becky... No night. No Afghanistan. No blood.

Justin kneeled over Becky's torso. How long had he been like that? Frozen and spaced out in another time... Long enough for Matt to get inside with a gurney and oxygen. Justin gave himself a shake.

"We've got to turn her over. Get her on O-2," Matt said. "Her breathing is erratic."

"Right." Justin nodded, knowing he should have been the one saying that. A doctor taking orders from a medic—if that wasn't a slap in the face, he didn't know what was. "On three. One. Two. Three."

They turned Becky to her left side and lifted her over the gurney pad. Her eyes flickered open and she looked up at him.

"Where's Tommy?" Her eyelids fluttered restlessly then closed.

Tommy? Justin fought waves of strong emotions pressing over him at the mention of his backstabbing former friend. Becky knew Tommy Kirkpatrick? How was that for irony?

"Relax, Becky. You're going to be fine," he said.

Matt eyed him for a second, then they both continued to ready her for the trip to the hospital. Justin put away his wandering thoughts and tried to focus on his work. He'd given medical attention to Afghani, to insurgents and to plenty of soldiers he didn't particularly care for. He hardly knew Becky. Why should this be different. Right?

Matt secured Becky to the gurney. Justin grabbed the oxygen tank and placed the tubing around her face. Even pale and semiconscious, she was breathtakingly beautiful.

Focus, soldier. Again, he seized his errant thoughts. Patient. She's a patient. Not a beautiful woman he'd just had a pleasant conversation with. She was no one. Anyone. Same as all the other patients. He touched her face to place the tubing. Her eyes opened again. Her body contracted, fighting against the restraints Matt had used to secure her legs on the gurney.

"Don't try to move," he said to her.

"I took your coffee." She looked up at him. Her fingers wrapped around his wrist. Her hand was cold, but her long fingers shot a rush of heat through Justin's skin. Right. Just like all the other patients.

He pulled his hand away and took his position at the head of the gurney ready to help Matt wheel her out and get her into the van.

As they passed through the foyer, Justin glanced around the room, wondering why Tommy wasn't there. He guessed Becky must be his girlfriend. The Tommy he remembered had always been able to get any girl he wanted. Although it was hard to imagine Tommy dating a schoolteacher and even harder to imagine Aggie Kirkpatrick's approval of such a liaison. Last he'd heard, Tommy lived in Atlanta and was working for some Fortune Five Hundred company.

And wasn't that exactly where Becky had said she was from? He sighed as they made their way down the front walk. Sometimes life seemed too cruel.

"Wait." Mrs. Kirkpatrick raced out of the house after them. "Where are you taking her?"

"To the hospital," Justin said.

"But…is that a good idea? I mean, is it okay to move her?" Aggie looked frantic.

Justin studied the woman, gazing down at the younger one lying down on the gurney. Never before had he seen Aggie show such concern over another human being. His eyes grew wide at her uncharacteristic behavior. She almost looked fearful. He remembered Matt's words about one of the Kirkpatrick family having passed away. Tommy?

No. Not Tommy.

Matt pulled the gurney toward the van. "She needs to go to the hospital, ma'am. Her breathing isn't stable. We'll take her to University Hospital."

"But…" Aggie hesitated, looking from Matt to Justin then back to Matt. "She's—she's pregnant."

Pregnant? Justin swallowed hard. That's why the gardener had said *bambino.*

"How far along?" Matt asked.

"Five months."

Justin glanced over Becky's long, slender figure. Even now, lying on her back, there was only the slightest indication that she carried a baby. In the coffee shop, the flowing cut of her long dress and jacket had hidden her shape completely. But really, how could a doctor not notice that a woman was five months pregnant? Maybe he hadn't wanted to notice.

Strange emotions swirled through Justin, emotions he did not welcome. He tried to shake the unwanted feelings from his head and focus on helping a patient, whose past, present and future should not affect his job in any way. But this woman possibly carried Tommy's child. And that news felt like a knife in his chest.

"Don't worry, ma'am." Matt glanced back at Mrs. Kirkpatrick. "We'll take great care of your daughter-in-law."

Justin followed Matt to the emergency vehicle, trying to absorb the whole truth—that Becky wasn't only a friend of Tommy's, she was his wife and they were expecting a child. So what? Why did that news bother him? It shouldn't.

But it did. On so many levels, he couldn't even begin to sort through all of the things he was feeling.

They lifted the gurney into the back of the van. Becky's eyelids quivered again, but she didn't speak. Justin closed the back doors, hurried around to the driver's side and started the engine. Matt stayed in back to monitor her.

Once they were on the road, Matt tapped on the divider between the front and the back of the van and yelled to be heard over the loud engine. "What happened back there? Are you okay?"

Justin kept his eyes on the road. What *had* happened back there? He'd flashed back to his living nightmare and had seen blood where there had been none. He'd discovered the man he disliked most in the world had married the most beautiful woman he'd ever seen and they were having a baby together. It was a lot to take in.

"That's her," Justin said, trying to sound calm and collected. "That's the woman I met in the coffee shop. The one I was telling you about earlier."

"Wow. That *is* weird. But seriously? Is that the reason you froze? Because this lady smiled at you in a coffee shop?"

Right. Justin's teeth clenched. He wished it were that simple. But he knew as well as Matt did that wasn't all that was going on. He hardly knew Becky. And now that he found out she was a Kirkpatrick, he didn't want to know her. The Kirkpatricks had broken his family, and used them without looking back. Justin wanted no part of them or anyone associated with them. Nor did he want to think of the strange emotions coursing through him when he glanced at her.

And then there was this panicking thing he did. It was more serious than he'd thought. His stupid head was playing tricks on him. Drawing up images of Gentry. And insurgents. And fear that felt so real it *became* real. In his mind, anyway. Frustration flooded through him. He'd really hoped the episodes would stop once he was stateside. But he'd been wrong. Coming home wasn't going to be the quick cure he'd believed it would be.

This was turning out to be one lousy afternoon.

"Can't we talk about this later? How's she doing?" Justin asked, wanting more time to think about the panic attack before he discussed it.

"She's stable," Matt said. "I don't know about the baby. I don't have a fetal doppler on board, so I can't listen for a heartbeat."

A riveting ache rushed through Justin. Kirkpatrick or not, he didn't want this woman to lose her baby. He and Tommy weren't friends anymore but he could never want something like that to happen to anyone, not even to Tommy. No matter what the Kirkpatricks had done to him and his family.

"So when did Tommy move back to Glendale?" Justin asked.

"Man, you really don't know, do you?"

"I don't know what?" Justin glanced at his friend in the rearview mirror.

"Tommy Kirkpatrick is dead."

Chapter Three

Becky awoke to voices and traffic sounds. Her limbs lay heavy at her sides. Her eyelids felt thick and lazy. She forced them open, finding above her a bright blue sky, which she viewed from the flat of her back. Two men—one on each side of her—pushed her into a large building.

Glendale University Hospital. Paramedics were rushing her to the hospital. Why? What had happened? Tears pooled in her eyes. A burst of adrenaline flooded through her. She tried to reach a hand to her belly, but her arm met resistance.

Not the baby, Lord. Please not my baby. Please don't take away the baby, too.

A few tears escaped the corners of her eyes.

Becky closed her lids, pressing out the rest of the tears. *Please, Lord. Give me courage. Don't take away the one thing I have left. Peace, Lord. Bring peace to my heart.*

But it had been so long since Becky had felt peace she could hardly remember what it felt like. She tried to sit up. A gentle hand on her shoulder kept her in place against the hard gurney. Becky looked into a pair of warm chocolate-colored eyes.

"Be still. We'll get you to a more comfortable place in a minute." Becky recognized the kind eyes, staring into hers.

The man was Justin Winters, the medic from the coffee shop. His angular face and day-old stubble were pretty easy on the eyes, even ones full of tears. The familiarity and sweetness of his expression slowed Becky's racing heart. She took a deep breath. "I don't remember what happened. I had a cramp and then…"

He nodded, but didn't look down at her again.

"It's okay," he said. "You're going to be fine. Don't try to talk. You need all of your oxygen."

Oxygen. She noticed the tubing around her mouth and nose. She felt the strain as she tried to inhale. And just like that, the panic returned. "Why? What happened? What about my…" Becky gasped for precious air. Speaking was too difficult. Plus, she didn't want to say what she might have lost. Without air, she became weak and light-headed, as if one more word would cause her to faint away. She closed her eyes and bit into her lower lip. Was that what had happened at Aggie's? She'd fainted—had she run out of air? But why? She'd been breathing fine then. Right?

Slowly she remembered the episode in Aggie's living room. The pain. The cramping in her abdomen. And the tears came harder now. She should have taken better care of herself. She shouldn't have shut down after Tommy's death and grieved for so long. She shouldn't have moved in with Tommy's mother. It was too hard. Tommy had thought it would be good, that it would provide her with the home he'd had to leave, but he hadn't realized the emotional strain moving to Glendale would cause on her and her body.

Justin did not respond to her, nor did he look at her again as they slipped through the double sliding doors into the ER. Computer noises and people replaced the sounds of traffic. A sterile, antiseptic-like odor filled Becky's head and made her queasy. She closed her eyes, trying to disregard the nauseating movement of the gurney as they rolled her along.

"The doctors will be able to give you a more thorough exam. But we have no reason to think there is anything wrong." The other medic gave her a halfhearted smile.

Becky stared back at him. Who was he kidding? There *was* something wrong. He just didn't know what. The sooner she saw the doctor, the better.

"Stop. Stop, right there." A woman's voice spoke from across the room.

Becky's eyes flew open as the gurney came to an abrupt halt. Her head turned toward the woman's voice. A short, round lady in a lab coat, clutching a large clipboard to her chest, approached at warp speed.

"We're Glendale Medical Team. We called in." Justin spread his weight on both legs and stood tall, like a stone barrier between Becky and the woman.

"I know you called in, but the E.R. is full." She snorted and pulled a pencil from behind her ear. "The dispatcher was supposed to tell you to go to County."

"Well, they didn't, and we're here." Becky could hear a sharp edge to Justin's voice that bordered on fierceness. "This woman is pregnant and she needs to see a doctor stat."

"It will take hours for her to be admitted here. Our E.R. nurses are on strike."

Strike? What kind of nurses went on strike? Becky noticed that Justin seemed to be wondering the same thing as the muscles in his neck and cheek flexed in irritation. He turned to his partner. "How far is County?"

"Twenty minutes. But it's not a real hospital. They aren't equipped for major emergencies," Matt said.

Becky couldn't believe this. They were going to turn her and her baby away? This couldn't be happening. Weren't there laws against this sort of thing? Short, ineffective breaths started to rack her chest and shake the gurney. What if something was wrong with her baby? Would they really risk moving her to another facility?

Justin glanced down. A reluctant compassion filled his eyes and he softly placed a hand to her shoulder. "Slow, Becky. Slow breaths." His touch was warm and soothed her edginess.

Justin turned back to the woman blocking their entry. "She's going to go into respiratory arrest. She's five months pregnant. Do you want that on your conscience? Do you even know who she is?"

"I don't care who she is. And it's not on my conscience. I'm not on strike.… Look, I've got thirty-three emergencies in here. If you're not bleeding out, you're going to be waiting. The best thing you can do is get back in your van and take her to County." The woman started to turn away.

Justin took two long steps after the lady and stopped her with a hand on her shoulder. She swung around to face him, looking more frustrated than ever. But Justin calmly leaned over her and whispered something close to her face.

The woman's eyes widened as she stepped back. The tight muscles in her face began to relax. "Oh. Well. Why didn't you say so? I'll have someone from the third floor come down with a transfer bed. Just wait over here to the side. Won't be a second."

Justin and the other medic wheeled her farther down a wide corridor. Thanks to whatever Justin had said, they were going to admit her. Soon she'd find out if her baby was going to be okay.

"Thank you," she whispered to him.

Justin glanced down at her with a cold look. "Just doing my job."

Becky closed her eyes again, shutting out the image of

Justin's icy gaze. He suddenly seemed like a very different man than the one she'd met at the coffee shop. Instead, she concentrated on her breathing—slow and steady. In. Out.

I can't lose my baby, too, she thought to herself as she floated out of consciousness again.

Justin watched as the third-floor nurse rolled Becky Kirkpatrick away to get the care she needed. He should have been more encouraging to her, made sure she felt relaxed and safe. Justin had always prided himself on being a good doctor, on being able to put aside his own needs and thoughts and get to his work without distraction or delay. But today he hadn't done that and it made his insides twist. Especially as he had no idea if his bad attitude and panic attack had been caused by the PTSD or his dislike of the Kirkpatricks. Maybe it was some combination of the two.

"Come on, man." Matt spun the gurney around behind him. "Let's get our paperwork and get out of here. This place is crazy."

Justin turned slowly, his head reeling with all the information and events it had processed in the past twenty minutes. Reeling until it stopped at the name Kirkpatrick.

Tommy Kirkpatrick was a person Justin hadn't allowed himself to think about in years. Twelve years, to be exact.

He looked to Matt. "How did—how did Tommy die?"

"Leukemia. He couldn't tolerate the chemo."

Tommy. The two of them had parted ways long ago and on such terrible terms. Still, the news of his death should have moved Justin, made him sad or gratified or something. Instead, Justin felt empty. Dead himself. And really, why was he even asking about Tommy's death? It was like asking about a stranger. Right?

Matt punched him playfully in the arm. "So, that was

great how you got her admitted. How did you get that lady to change her mind?"

"What?" Justin released a deep sigh. He looked up at Matt as they pushed the gurney back to the emergency van. "What lady?"

"The administrator lady. You told her you're a doctor, didn't you?"

"Uh." Justin looked away. "Yeah, I did."

Matt nodded.

"And that I'd help out in the E.R."

Matt threw his head back, laughing. "You're kidding?"

"Nope. I volunteered."

"You're going to work in that overcrowded E.R.? For free? Are you crazy?"

Maybe. "No. I'm not crazy. I figured—what's a couple of hours, you know? Help them weed through the people and Becky gets admitted. It's a win-win." That is, if he could actually do the work without panicking and having flashbacks.

Matt looked back at him with a skeptical expression.

"Look, I just wanted to get her admitted. It seemed like the least I could do after…hesitating the way I did."

"Hesitating?"

"How bad was it?" Justin's face pinched. He couldn't be getting worse, could he?

"You were pretty frozen in place. You think that will happen again? Do you think you're up for the E.R.?"

Justin shrugged. "I don't know. I guess I'll have to be."

"Or?" Matt narrowed his eyes. "You could take a few more days off."

"No." Justin wiped his hand over his face, hoping it covered the confusion that must have been glazing over his eyes. "She needed to be admitted. And I need to get past this. The sooner, the better. I'm gonna get over this, Matt. I am."

"Look, I don't know what happened to you in the Middle East, but you don't have to push yourself so hard," Matt said.

They reached the van. Matt folded the gurney, slid it back inside and shut the doors.

Justin handed him the van keys but blocked his path back to the driver's side. "Yes. Actually, I do have to push myself."

"Fine. I get that. I'd be the same way." Matt scratched his head and looked down at the radio clipped to his belt. "In fact, you know what? I've got my radio right here. I can leave if someone needs me, but in the meantime, how about I come inside with you and help out in the E.R., too?"

"Sounds good. Even though without hospital privileges we can't do much more than hand out bandages."

Matt laughed and slapped him on the back. "But that beats watching talk shows and waiting for a call."

"Exactly," Justin said, praying he could do the work he'd just volunteered for.

After a series of blood tests, physical exams and a bag of IV fluids, Becky regained some strength. A vivacious nurse helped her into a wheelchair and rolled her quickly to ultrasound. Finally, she would see if the baby was okay. Actually, Dr. Klein had already assured her the baby was fine, but until Becky could see the proof with her own eyes, she couldn't seem to quiet the worry and doubts swimming inside her.

She unfolded the blanket over her hospital gown and turned her head to the nurse who had apparently been speaking to her. "I'm sorry. Did you ask me something?"

"How many weeks?" the nurse repeated. "You're hardly showing."

"Twenty-three. And, yes, I am showing. I think the hospital gown is camouflage."

The woman laughed. "I've heard hospital gowns called lots of things but never camouflage. Girl or boy?"

"Oh. I don't know. I haven't had an ultrasound before. In any case, we..." Becky stopped and swallowed hard. "I didn't want to find out." Actually, it had been Tommy who didn't want to learn the sex. Becky stared down at her hands fidgeting in her lap.

"Well, don't look at the screen," the nurse warned. "At twenty-three weeks, it should be pretty obvious. How about names? Do you and your husband have any names picked out?"

Husband. No.

Names. No.

Becky pressed her lips together. She and Tommy had never had a chance to discuss that subject. She lifted her head. "No. Not yet."

"Okay, here we are. Ultrasound."

The technician was quick with her pictures. But for a few glorious moments, as she waved the ultrasound reading instrument over her tummy, Becky could hear the soft whirring sounds of her baby's heartbeat and she could see a foot, a hand, a face and that the baby was a girl. Tears of relief flooded her eyes as she listened and watched. *Thank you, Lord. Thank You for this life. For this little girl.*

The technician pulled off her latex gloves and put away the wand. "I'm going to call the doctor down. He wanted to look at the pictures and meet with you in here."

By the time Becky had managed to tie up the back of that ridiculous hospital gown, Dr. Klein was looking through the images the technician had left for him on the monitor. Afterward, he sat down on a stool near her, folded his hands together and took a deep breath. His face creased deeply with stress lines around his eyes and mouth.

Becky squirmed on the exam table. If there was bad news, best to just get it said. "So, what's wrong?"

"You have gestational diabetes."

"I do? Since when?

"Well, hard to say, but it's always diagnosed at this point in a pregnancy. So don't worry. It's not due to any negligence on your part."

"Is it dangerous for the baby?"

"It shouldn't be. The main things we want to watch for are a premature delivery and excess growth. Of course, you'll have to follow a strict diet. And watch your blood sugars. But with proper monitoring, both you and the baby will be fine. And the diabetes will probably disappear with the pregnancy."

"And that's what caused the cramping and my passing out?"

Dr. Klein tilted his head slowly from one side to the other. "It is definitely why you passed out. And I think it caused you to become dehydrated, which caused the cramping. From now on we will be monitoring your pregnancy very closely."

Becky took in his calming words, surprised herself that she wasn't more upset about the report. But she wasn't. For some reason, after seeing the pictures of her baby, she felt more secure than she had in months. And she liked the idea of the doctor keeping a close watch over her and the baby. "How closely?"

"Ultrasounds every few weeks. And checkups, too. And Becky, Mrs. Kelly told me that you've been staying at home all the time since you moved to Glendale. Is that true?"

She nodded. "I don't know anyone. Where would I go?"

"Anywhere. Outside. For a walk. For a drive. Fresh air

and exercise are important in any pregnancy but even more so when you have gestational diabetes."

Becky smiled. "Are you saying I need to get out more?"

"Yes." He grinned. "I know your mother-in-law will not like me telling you that. I'm sure she's ready to order a private nurse for you and keep you under lock and key. I'd imagine you gave her a good scare today."

"But the baby is fine, right?"

"The baby looks perfect. And I want to keep it that way. But I think you'll be healthier and the baby will be healthier with a little more fresh air and a little less time…"

"Being sad." Becky pressed her lips together.

"Yes."

Becky knew he was right. It was depressing being in that big empty house all day long. And when was the last time she'd been to church? "I agree I could use a little more fresh air." But would Aggie let her do anything? "You're right though, Aggie's not going to like it."

"If she has any questions after you talk to her, I'll be glad to answer them."

"I have a question."

"Sure." Dr. Klein smiled down at her.

"Would it be okay for me to take a teaching position for a few weeks? Part-time."

"If you can spend some of the time seated, yes. I don't see why not."

"And the cramps?"

"I don't think you'll have those anymore, as long as you're careful with your diet and make sure to stay hydrated. Of course, if you do you need to tell me right away. Don't wait for the next appointment. And listen to me when I say this is nothing you can't get through. You're a strong person. I knew that when I first met you." He stood from the stool and walked toward the door. "Now, get some rest. We're keeping you overnight so that we can monitor your blood sugar a little longer. I'll check on you the first thing in the morning and then you can go home and get on with things."

Get on with things. He made it sound so simple.

Chapter Four

"Need a ride back to the station?" Matt wiped beads of sweat from his brow, the result of six hours of non-stop work in the overcrowded E.R.

"No. I'm good." Justin pulled his cell from his pocket and waved it at Matt. "I'll call Katie. She's driving me around until I get my Jeep up and running again. But thanks."

In the late afternoon sun, Matt looked as tired as Justin felt. His friend staggered around to the driver's side of the van and drove away from the hospital. Justin hit the speed-dial number for his sister and leaned against the brick columns of the E.R. hospital entrance. He did need a ride home, but he had a few other things to take care of, too.

Number one, it seemed he had a new temporary employment in the hospital clinic. The difficult woman from Administration, so thrilled with his offer to help in the E.R. and so careful to check out his credentials, was able to get him hospital privileges in less than an hour. So, he had not handed out bandages in the E.R., as he'd anticipated. He and Matt had treated everything from acute appendicitis to broken ribs to small lacerations. The six hours in the chaotic E.R. had worn him down, but boosted his confidence at the same time. He did experience flash images of desert and rebels and flaming planes, but one look at Matt or one thought of Becky Kirkpatrick and her hospital admittance and Justin was able to focus on the task at hand.

He hoped this would be the beginning of the end of his panic attacks. Not to mention, between a job in the clinic and helping his sister out at the school in the afternoons, he could stay busy enough to forget he even had a problem. Maybe.

"Katie," Justin said into his cell phone. "Matt left me at the hospital. Can you pick me up after school?"

"It *is* after school," his sister said. "Why did Matt leave you at the hospital?"

"We had a call and I decided to see about working at the clinic while I was here." Justin thought he'd leave out the details about the Kirkpatricks and the ER and his panic attack.

"Sure, I can pick you up," she said. "So, how'd it go?"

"How did what go?" Justin tensed.

"The ambulance. How did it go? Must be pretty boring after the Middle East."

"Oh. Well, not so boring. But okay… Well, it could have gone better. Why didn't anyone…" *Tell me about Tommy? Why don't I just shut up before she figures out how upset I am?* His head was spinning again with images of blood and Becky and Gentry and—

"You okay, Justin?"

No. "Yep. I'm fine."

"I'll be there in about fifteen."

"Great." Justin folded his phone and slid it back into his pocket before going back to fill out the paperwork in the clinic. They were so excited to have him, they handed him a doctor's pass and asked him to start working the next day.

Now, Justin stood in the elevator with his finger hovering over the button to the third floor where he knew Becky had been admitted. It seemed like a stupid thing to do, to go see her. But he wanted to find out if his hesitation had caused her any problems. Kirkpatrick or not, he couldn't stand the thought that his own problems could have hurt another person. He had to know if she was okay. And really, that wasn't the same as going to *see* her, he was merely inquiring about her condition. That was totally different. In fact, once he knew she was fine, he would leave. He didn't even need to talk to her.

He pressed the button to the third floor and approached the nurses' station. Hopefully, his medic uniform and his new doctor's pass would allow him some information, even if he wasn't the doctor assigned to her case.

"Hello. I was on the team that brought in Mrs. Kirkpatrick. I wanted to check on her status, if I could." Justin leaned over the large counter. Two women writing notes in patient files completely ignored him. Justin cleared his throat. "Mrs. Kirkpatrick? She was admitted a few hours ago?"

The older of the two nurses looked up, eyed his medic uniform looking very unimpressed and pointed down the hallway behind him. "Mrs. Kirkpatrick? She's coming your way. Ask her yourself."

Coming my way? Justin glanced over his shoulder. The woman didn't lie. Becky Kirkpatrick was in a quickly approaching wheelchair, which a nurse pushed right up beside him, parked and pulled the brake. *Great.* Exactly what he'd hoped to avoid.

"I'll be right back, Mrs. Kirkpatrick," the nurse said. "I'm just going to put your file away."

Becky nodded as the nurse stepped away, accidentally pulling the blanket that covered Becky's legs with her. Becky's eyes grew impossibly wide and she grabbed desperately at the dark coverlet but her hands were not fast enough.

The blanket had somehow stuck to the files the nurse carried and there it went along with her to the nurses' station.

Forgetting his plan not to interact with her, Justin reached over and grabbed the blanket from the nurse, who seemed clueless of the situation she'd created.

"Here." He handed the blanket to her.

"Thanks." She fidgeted in her chair, covering her legs quickly and carefully then looked up at him.

"So, we meet again," she said.

"For the third time." Justin tried to swallow, but his mouth felt dry and his heart beat hard against his chest like he'd just finished a ten-mile run. "I'm surprised you remember."

"I remember the coffee shop," she said. "I took your drink order. But I'll be honest. I don't really remember the second meeting."

"No, I don't imagine that you do." He smiled, in spite of himself. "I hope you're feeling better?"

"Yes, thank you. Good as new."

"Great. Glad to hear it. I came to check."

"Well, thanks. That was nice of you." She waved a dismissive hand through the air.

He tilted his head away, feeling rejected. Not that that should surprise him. Dismissing members of the Winters family was what Kirkpatricks did best. But he couldn't just walk away. He was a doctor. He wanted to know more. Like why had she passed out. And what had happened to the baby? Maybe he wanted to know everything. "So, your doctor has you all fixed up? You're not going to pass out anymore?"

"But I thought you liked that." She grinned. "I recently heard that the medics in Glendale were bored. I was just trying to help out."

"Bored?" Justin lifted a hand to his forehead as he felt the warmth flow into his cheeks. "Ack. I did say that, didn't I?"

"Something like that."

"Let me be more clear, then. Boring is good."

"Don't worry. I don't plan on any more episodes like that. Turns out I have gestational diabetes. I should be fine with a change in my diet."

"Ah. Your blood sugar was a little off?"

"Way off."

"Good, then." Justin closed his eyes at the stupid remark. "Well, not good that you have gestational diabetes. I meant good that it's not… Sorry. It's just that you were so pale… And your—your—" He couldn't seem to pronounce the word *baby*.

"The baby is fine," she said quickly.

"So why the overnight?" He was asking too many questions but he couldn't seem to stop himself.

"I'm just staying one night so Dr. Klein can watch my blood sugars."

Justin wished he could disappear into the awkward silence that followed. Why hadn't he just left when she'd dismissed him? Or, why couldn't she have already been in the room so he could have simply asked the nurse some questions and avoided this scene? He began to back away. "Great. That's great… I'm glad you're better. Take care."

"Thanks. I do appreciate you coming by. I don't know many people in town."

Justin looked back. She was smiling but in her eyes Justin saw pain and fear as deep as his own. He paused. Should he say he was sorry for her loss? Tell her that he was her husband's best friend for most of his life and not some random stranger from a coffee shop? No. Apparently, the name Winters didn't mean anything to her. No need to change that. If she knew a little, she'd want to know more and that would… Well, that would be bad for everyone. So, he should leave. And he should do so quickly. Before he said more. Before he felt more. This woman did something to his insides. Something he did not like at all.

He forced a smile. "Glendale is a small town. You'll know everyone soon enough."

"So true, Dr. Winters. This is a small town." The nurse walked back behind Becky's wheelchair, undid the brake and looked down at Becky with a playful grin. "Except that your doctor here doesn't remember me even though he took me to high school homecoming one year."

"I did?" Justin blanched. "Right. Right. You're Katie's friend. Um…uh. Meredith."

"Melodie." The nurse looked at Becky again, pretending to be offended. "Melodie Barnes. Soon to be Melodie Abrams."

Becky watched the exchange carefully, the nurse enjoying the fact she'd caught Justin's forgetfulness and Justin squirming under her faux chastisement.

"Sorry. I'm bad with names, Melodie." Then he gave her a smile that would have melted any woman into a puddle.

"Oh." She touched a hand to his arm. "I was just playing with you, Dr. Winters. I hardly would have expected you to remember me. But I see Katie all the time. I knew you were back in town."

Doctor? The woman had said that twice now. Doctor. Medic. Pilot. Who was this guy? And for the record, Becky didn't approve of the way the nurse was touching him. It was a little too friendly. Hadn't she said she was getting married soon?

"Yes, just got back." Justin shot a furtive glance down at Becky in the wheelchair. His eyes said he was nervous about something. Perhaps all the confusion about his profession. Well, she wasn't going to let him off the hook.

"So now you're a doctor?" Becky asked.

Melodie giggled, as if Becky had just said the stupidest thing possible. "Justin's not just a doctor. He's a flight surgeon. And one of the best."

A flight surgeon pretending to be a medic. Becky lifted an eyebrow. It seemed Justin Winters had a story of his own. One day when she wasn't so tired maybe she'd like to hear it. But for now, she needed rest and some time to reflect on how she might approach Aggie about her new job and her medical condition. And she needed even more time to release the dreaded fear in her mind—the one that told her over and over that she would lose everything, just as she had with her mother and Tommy. It was all just a matter of time….

Becky settled back in her new hospital bed on the third floor and glanced over at Aggie, sitting across from her with her head down working a crossword puzzle. Her mind kept popping back to that last encounter with Justin Winters. A doctor. Why hadn't he said so from the beginning? And why was he working as a medic? It was like he was hiding something from her and he didn't seem the type. Of course, what did she know about him? Little to nothing. And more importantly, why did she care?

She turned her attention back to Aggie. Weariness showed in the woman's slumped shoulders and her slightly unkempt hair. Becky felt fatigued as well but she needed to talk to Aggie. It wouldn't be easy, but if she wanted to keep her promise to Tommy, things would have to change at the Kirkpatrick house.

She took a few sips from her ice water then placed it back on to the tray table in front of her. "It was really sweet of Mrs. Kelly to be here today." Mrs. Kelly had driven Aggie to the hospital, and had stayed with her until Becky was given her room for the night.

Aggie lifted her head. "I'd have done the same for her. In fact, I have on many an occasion."

"Well, you're blessed to have such a good friend." Becky accentuated the words. For once, she was going to direct the course of conversation between them. "I miss my friends in Atlanta. I could certainly use their support right now. Phone calls aren't the same as face-to-face."

What little color was left in Aggie's face seemed to drain away. "Are you saying you want to move back to Atlanta? I don't think that's what is best for you and this baby. You can hardly take care of yourself. You need constant care. What if you were to pass out again?"

"Aggie, I told you what Dr. Klein said. You know I don't need constant care and with my new diet I won't be passing out anymore."

Aggie looked indignant. "Well, I suppose if I haven't made it clear before, I think you should stay at least until the baby is born. It's what Tommy wanted."

Her words sounded cold, but Becky took them at face value. Aggie was reaching out. It was a first. And maybe a start to what Tommy had really wanted. "It *is* what Tommy wanted. And I agree I don't really want to pack up and move again. I like Dr. Klein and I like living with you." *Sometimes,* she wanted to add. "But you and I need to set a few ground rules if I'm going to stay in your home for another four to five months."

Aggie stood from the chair and stepped toward the bedside, folding her arms across her chest. "I already told you that I would be happy to let you redecorate the rooms you're living in."

"No. That's not it." Becky sat up tall in the bed.

"What then?"

"Well, I talked with Dr. Klein and he and I both agree

that I've spent too much time at the house. He says I can take the teaching job. So that's my first condition."

"But Rebecca." Aggie shook her head in protest. "After what happened today, I think—"

"Aggie, if you can't agree to the conditions, then I don't think I can stay with you. As hard as this is, I have to move on with my life and that means getting out and meeting people, finding a church, making friends my own age," she said. "I need this. It's not healthy for me to hide away in your house and therefore, it's not good for the baby."

"Getting out of the house once or twice a week, sure. But working? I'm having a hard time believing that Dr. Klein would want you to take a job."

"Believe it. And remember, it's part-time. Afternoons only. And only for a few weeks while the other teacher is on her own maternity leave. That's nothing. I have about fifteen more weeks of this pregnancy."

Aggie's jaw clenched tight. "I'm going to discuss this with Dr. Klein."

Becky smiled. "I think that's a great idea."

Aggie grabbed up her purse and headed for the door.

"Wait. I wasn't finished."

"There's another condition?" Aggie turned back and folded her arms again.

Becky smiled. It felt nice to have a little power in this relationship for a change. And the fact that Aggie was even listening meant that she cared, way more than she'd ever shown or said. "Yes. I want to take the job and I want a little more freedom in the house."

"You're as free as a bird." Aggie waved a hand through the air.

Becky knew she was pushing her mother-in-law but she had to. It was time. "Maybe it seems that way but the nine o'clock breakfast, the twelve-thirty lunch, the six-thirty dinner… I'd like to just eat when I'm hungry. Fix my own meals. Buy some of my own groceries even. Come and go from the house without worrying that you'll wait for me or worry."

"Well, if you don't like Dyanna's cooking why didn't you say so? And I suppose you don't like any of the clothes I've bought for you, either. I understand we have different tastes." She turned away. "Don't worry. The dress you wore today was ruined. You won't have to wear it again."

"Oh, Aggie." Becky grunted in frustration. "You're missing the point. I love Dyanna's cooking. And you have fabulous taste in clothes. But I miss making decisions for myself. I'm an adult. I need to have that back."

"And that's it?" Aggie looked stern as if one more condition would be the deal breaker.

But Becky was determined. She was going for broke. "No, there's one other condition."

"I can't even imagine what it might be," Aggie said. "You know this is very ungrateful of you."

Becky was afraid Aggie would feel that way, but without pushing a little, Aggie would never change. *Lord, make me strong and wise beyond my years so that this woman can see You.* "I know this must seem ungrateful to you. But Aggie, nothing could be further from the truth. I have been so thankful for your presence and your help. I don't know how I would have gotten through the last few months without your help and support. You're the only one who loved Tommy as much as I did. The only one who could understand the loss the way that I do.

"So Aggie, this last condition is from Tommy. It has to do with his wishes. He wanted me to stay with you until the baby is born, but he wanted me to go on with my life. That's all I'm trying to do by the things that I've asked. Not be ungrateful. That's the furthest thing from my mind. And

Tommy wanted something else…something from you…well, from both of us."

Aggie sighed as if annoyed, but Becky could tell her words had softened the woman. More likely, she was nervous about the request from her son, because Tommy was some-one she could not easily refuse. "What else could Tommy have wanted? I think it was a lot that he wanted me to open my home. After all, you and I hardly know each other."

Becky pressed her lips together, letting the cutting words slide away. Aggie didn't mean them and they both knew it. She took a deep breath and looked Tommy's mother in the eye. "Tommy wanted us to attend church together."

"Well, if that doesn't beat all." Aggie's eyes went wide at first then she restored the normal stoic facade. A silence fell between them and Becky began to worry that perhaps she'd pushed the church thing too soon. She and Aggie weren't close, but the woman was still a tie connecting her to Tommy. She'd lost so much of him already—she couldn't bear to lose more if Aggie took offense and refused to give in to Becky's demands.

"You know, Aggie, I take that back. I can't make church a condition. That's unfair. No one should be forced to seek God. But if I stay, I'll be attending myself. And it would make me very happy if we could go together."

Another silence fell. This one longer than the first. Then, at length, Aggie headed back to the door where she paused, straightened her torso and set her jaw. "It's settled, then. We'll visit Community Church this Sunday. Mrs. Fitzwil-liams attends there. Been inviting me for years. She'll be so happy, I don't know if either of us will be able to stand it…. Get some rest, Rebecca. I'll be back in the morning to take you home."

Becky stared at the closed door for a long moment after Aggie had departed, unable to grasp her mother-in-law's compliance. Then, exhausted, she slid back against the deep pillows of the hospital bed and released some of her anxiety. In its place came a glimmer of new hope. Not much, but just enough to lighten her heart and allow her to fall off into a peaceful sleep.

Chapter Five

Becky collapsed into the desk chair at the sound of the final school bell. Twenty-four sixth graders filed out of her room hollering about video games, baseball practice, dance lessons and too much homework. Slowly, their voices faded from the hallway and there was silence again. Becky didn't like the silence. That was when her mind wandered. That was when sadness and doubt stole her peace and took up residence in her heart.

Lord, fill those silent spaces in me. The ones that feel so empty. Fill them with something good. Fill them with love and peace.

She let out a deep sigh and pressed her mind to think on good things, like what a blessing it was to have all these children in her life. And how great she'd felt since starting her new diet a few days ago. A smile tugged at her mouth as she began to straighten her desk, gathering the stacks of papers she needed to grade for tomorrow.

"Becky Kirkpatrick?"

Startled, Becky dropped the papers from her hands as a woman appeared in her classroom doorway. She was young, with dark hair and big brown eyes much like Justin's.

"Yes, that's right," Becky answered, looking down at the dropped papers, which she began to collect.

The woman stepped forward. "I'm Katie Winters. I teach reading classes, too. Right across the hall there."

Becky smiled. "I thought you might be. Your brother told me that you worked here."

Katie narrowed her eyes a fraction. "You—you know my brother? I thought you were new to town."

Becky closed in the few steps to Katie and reached out to shake her hand. "I am new. It's nice to meet you."

Katie barely touched Becky's hand. "How do you know my brother, Justin?"

Becky paused at Katie's reaction, or rather her overreaction. But then, the woman had seemed distant from the start. Very different from her brother. "I met him at the coffee shop last week." She tilted her head and chuckled. "Then I saw him again at the hospital."

Katie's eyes widened. "The hospital?"

"Long story." Becky didn't see the need to explain her medical history to Justin's sister. At the same time, it was hard to ignore the woman's huge attitude. Was this over-protectiveness, perhaps? Becky was tempted to reassure her that she had no interest in any man just now, while she was still recovering from Tommy's death. Instead, she tucked the smart remark away. "Is something wrong?"

"No. Sorry." She shook her head. "It's just that…well, you must know that… I mean, I suppose that Justin told you—"

"I told her what?" Justin leaned against the door frame, a tentative smile spread over his angular face. It was not the same smile Becky remembered from the coffee shop, nor the nervous one from the hospital visit. This smile had unspoken distance and a warning relayed in it. A warning for her or for his sister, she wondered. When their eyes met, it faded from his lips. His arms crossed over the green scrubs highlighted his tension, adding to that which already filled the room.

Katie didn't finish her sentence.

"So, how's the middle school these days?" Justin asked, breaking the silence.

"It's—" Katie and Becky both started to answer, then stopped.

"How's the medic business?" Becky countered. "Or were you a doctor today?" Her words sounded more cutting than she'd intended. But somehow she felt that was more due to the tension in the air than to the sound of her voice.

"I worked in the clinic today." Justin moved next to his sister with great stiffness. "Did you tell her about the play?"

Katie cleared her throat. "I was getting ready to do that before you interrupted."

Justin moved back toward the door. "Then I'll wait for you in the car. Great to see you, Becky."

Right. So great he was practically running out of the room.

Katie grabbed his arm before he reached the door. "You can wait here."

Becky frowned. What was up with these two? They seemed so nervous. And over her, which made no sense. She sighed aloud. "Actually, I already know about the play. They told me when they hired me that the woman I was replacing had signed up to codirect the sixth-grade play, and that I'd have to fill her slot. Is it starting soon?"

Katie turned back to her, with a wary expression. "Yes, it goes really fast. Only a few weeks to get ready. I wrote up a schedule." She handed Becky a packet of papers. "And I picked the play. It's a modern kid's version of *Cyrano de Bergerac*."

Becky smiled. "That should be cute."

"I'll hold auditions on Friday."

Becky thumbed through the pages Katie handed her. There were a lot of practices. She hoped she could handle the schedule and not overdo it. Aggie would not be happy. "Looks like you've thought of everything. Great. So, just tell me what you'd like me to do."

Katie avoided eye contact. "Well, nothing actually. Like you said, I've got it taken care of. And seeing as you're pregnant, I was going to tell you that you're not really obligated to help. Justin and I have it all under control. No one will know if you just come to the last few practices and stand up on the stage with me at the end. It will be fine."

"It won't be fine because I would know. This is part of my contract. I can't just pretend like I did the work if I didn't." Becky looked back and forth between the brother and sister.

"Don't look at me." Justin moved again toward the door. "I'm just building the set. Meet you at the car, Katie." He walked out.

"It's really not a big deal at all," Katie said, also moving toward the door. "Just look through the schedule and find the last three rehearsals. Those are the ones you'll not want to miss. Let me know if you have any questions. See you around." She slipped out of the room.

Becky looked at the play schedule in her hand. It looked like a solid production and it was clear she was expected to participate. Everywhere the name Fox had been scratched out and the name Kirkpatrick scribbled in its place. So why the bizarre offer from Katie and Justin? And why the strange behavior, as if they couldn't wait to get away from her?

Becky gathered up her things and headed out to the parking lot. She had to admit that she was exhausted after one day's work. And the strange vibe from Katie and Justin wasn't sitting well with her. Something was going on with them.

Why had Justin been so friendly at the coffee shop, even encouraging her to meet his sister, and now both of them acted so standoffish? It was very curious, almost as if she'd done something to upset them. But what? And why did it matter? They did not have to be great pals to work on the school play together. And that's what was going to happen. Becky had agreed to do all Mrs. Fox's work, and that's exactly what she would do. Katie and Justin would have to understand that.

The drive home was awkward. Justin wanted Katie to talk to him. Instead, she sat arms folded, staring out the windshield in silence. He had no idea what to say to her after that scene at the school. While he could understand why she didn't want to work with Tommy's wife, he did not get why she seemed mad at him. No way she could have seen how he actually felt about Becky. He'd done everything in his power to hide that. Almost to the point of being rude. He felt bad about that, but he did want to protect his sister. And himself. Kirkpatricks brought their family nothing but trouble.

The truth was he'd wanted to come in and visit with Becky. Since the hospital, he'd been worried about her. But he reminded himself that he had to keep his distance. He needed to focus on getting himself better so he could go back to his unit. He couldn't let himself get distracted from that goal. Not even by a beautiful widow with the sweetest smile he'd ever seen.

Anyway, regardless of his feelings, Katie was clearly upset. He tried to think of something to distract her.

"Are you so rattled you're not even going to mention that I got my old Jeep running again? We're riding in my old

Jeep! Can you believe it? It just started right up this morning like it hadn't been sitting in the driveway for eight years. Amazing, isn't it? Now we don't have to share a car for three months. Isn't that great?"

"Super." Katie exhaled and dropped her arms to her sides. "She doesn't know, does she?"

Justin decided to play dumb. "Who? Becky?"

"Of course, Becky. Becky Kirkpatrick. She doesn't know."

"How would she know about my Jeep?"

"Very funny. You know that's not what I'm talking about."

"I know." Justin cleared his throat. "And, no. I haven't exactly come right out and introduced myself as a former pal of Tommy's, if that's what you're asking."

"You didn't exactly tell me you'd met her, either."

"Maybe because no one bothered to tell me about Tommy's death."

Katie looked away. Her head dropped a little. "Mom thought you had enough to deal with."

"You forget what a small town this is. I was bound to find out. It would have been much nicer finding out from you than at the Kirkpatricks' on an emergency call to help Tommy's pregnant widow."

Katie swung around to face him. "So that's what she meant by meeting you at the hospital. What's wrong with her?"

Justin cut his eyes at his sister.

"Oh, right. You're not allowed to say."

"No, I'm not. But I will say she was in a pretty bad state. I was surprised to find her teaching this week."

"There's something seriously wrong with her?"

"She's pregnant and has some complications. I can't say more than that and you know it. But she is under the care of a very good doctor. I hope she'll be fine." Justin had no proof and no reason to speculate, but he was worried for her. He did not like that she still looked so tired. And sad.

"Well, I don't get why she acts like she doesn't know who we are."

"Because she doesn't know, Katie."

"And you don't think that's weird? Don't people talk about their pasts before they get married? You were his best friend and I was…we!l…I was…whatever, and… How can she not know who we are?"

"It was a long time ago. It wasn't like we were invited to the wedding." Justin gave a fake smile.

"Obviously not." She rolled her eyes. "But it's so awkward. I don't know how to deal with seeing her every day."

"She's not Tommy."

"No. It's worse. She married him. If it were Tommy back here, I could be angry, but with her, I don't know what to do."

Justin glared at Katie. "You feel compassion for a woman who's just lost her spouse and is trying to find her way. Don't transfer your anger to her. She had nothing to do with the past."

"Yeah. I guess. I'm not really angry anyway. I just don't want to think about that time in my life. And she's a reminder. The less I see of her, the happier I'll be. Don't you feel the same way?"

Justin couldn't think of anything to say.

"You *don't* feel the same way, do you?" she asked. "In fact, if I didn't know better, I'd think you kind of liked her. You were trying a little too hard back there to seem indifferent."

Justin swallowed hard. How did this get to be about him all of a sudden? "Come on, Katie, I didn't know who Becky was when I first met her. Then, an hour later, she was passed out in the back of the ambulance and Matt's telling me she's Tommy's pregnant wife and that Tommy is dead. So…I don't know what I think about it. Or her. In fact, I don't even *want* to think about her. I just—I just want to get back with my unit."

Katie's head dropped to her chest. "Sorry, Justin. You have so much to deal with."

He gripped her shoulder in a reassuring touch. "Nah. I'm fine. But tell me what to do about the play."

"What do you mean?"

"Well, won't it be awkward with the three of us working together?"

"It won't be the three of us working together."

"I don't know, Katie. She didn't exactly jump at your idea."

"Well, she will. She doesn't need to help with the play. I can do it myself."

Justin pressed his lips together. "Still, maybe it would be less difficult without me there. I know you have some parents who like to help with that sort of thing."

Katie narrowed her eyes at him. "Oh, so now you're trying to back out of helping me?"

"Not at all. I—I just thought…" Justin shook his head. "Never mind what I thought. I'm glad to help."

"Good, because I'm counting on it. It will be like old times. And anyway, if you don't, I won't ever see you, especially now that you got this old Jeep running again."

"Well, we'll see how reliable it is. I may be calling you for a ride still."

"I hope so." She shot him a warm smile. "And don't worry about Mrs. Tommy Kirkpatrick. If she's like any other teacher in the school, she'll be thrilled she doesn't have to help out with a play."

* * *

"You look pale again this morning." Aggie shook the newspaper from her spot at the head of the dining room table.

"Good morning, Aggie." Becky's sandals clicked as she crossed the parquet flooring and took her seat at the opposite end of the table. Between them sat a fat silver urn filled with dried flowers. It acted conveniently as both centerpiece and divider. "Actually, I'm feeling fine today. Perhaps you're not used to my normal coloring. I've always been on the pale side of white."

"Perhaps. Or, perhaps, working doesn't agree with you."

Becky remained silent as Dyanna poured her a hot cup of herbal tea.

"If you need to get out more, walking will do."

Dyanna glanced down at Becky with a playful look in her eyes. They both tucked away a smile. "I do take walks, Aggie. Every day. Around the grounds and even on the adjoining farm."

"When I was expecting, I took at least three a day. It kept me trim, too. You don't want to gain too much weight, you know."

"I don't think I've gained too much weight." She'd hardly gained any.

"Twenty pounds is plenty." Aggie was on a roll. There was no stopping her now.

Becky sucked in her cheeks and glanced down at her torso. She hardly looked pregnant. Aggie couldn't possibly mean what she was saying. Dyanna placed a bowl of steaming-hot oatmeal in front of her and gave her an encouraging wink. "Thanks, Dyanna."

"How much have you gained?"

"I—I don't know. I haven't had much of an appetite—"

"Well, I'll get a scale taken to your room right away." Aggie folded up the section of paper and laid it aside. She leaned around the centerpiece urn and looked Becky over. "Is this the new pants suit I ordered you from New York?"

"It is." Becky took a small bite of her meal.

"It's quite lovely. Although a little large through the chest, don't you think?"

Becky tried not to choke on her food. "I—I hadn't noticed that."

"Well, I could have Mrs. Chambers alter it for you."

"No, thank you. I think it fits just fine." Becky straightened the jacket of the New York designer outfit so that it sat squarely on her shoulders. "See? Really. I love it. It's perfect for work. Maybe a little dressier than most of the teachers, but—"

"Well, you can hardly be surprised you're dressed better than the other teachers. You are a Kirkpatrick now, living at Greyfield, after all, even if that's not what you're used to."

Here she goes. Becky refrained from rolling her eyes to the ceiling. Aggie loved to find ways to point out the fact that Becky's family had been poor. And that the Kirkpatricks were rich. That her father had run off and abandoned her. And that Tommy's father had run his own company. Of course, Tommy's father had also run off, but that didn't seem to count in Aggie's mind.

Tommy had never stood for his mother's snobbery, but whenever he hadn't been around, Aggie had found a way to draw the comparison into any conversation. Now that Tommy was gone, there was no one to rein her in. But that was Aggie. Always offering up opinions as facts. Becky sighed. She had no idea how she could talk to Aggie about her faith. She wondered if, when Sunday came, Aggie would actually go to church with her.

Lord, help me to love this woman. To be a witness to her as Tommy asked and as I know You would like.

When Becky refused to rise to the baited comments, they continued the breakfast in taut silence.

Becky longed for the soft voice of her own mother. How she missed her. How much would her presence have eased the loss of Becky's husband. She couldn't imagine that things could have ever felt so tense between the two of them. Her mother had always been slow to criticize and quick to smile. Sure, they'd had their disagreements, but there had always been this understanding between them—a bond of love and trust that surpassed petty dialogue and unfair judgments. Having been just the two of them, the bond had been strong. And then, only two months after leaving for college, Becky lost her to a stroke.

Losing Tommy had brought back that terrible grief in addition to the new sorrow. Sometimes, it felt as though God expected too much of her. She knew that wasn't true, but some days, like today, her burdens felt heavy. As did her heart. She tried to swallow down the dry lump in her throat. The fact that life moved on without Tommy seemed wrong somehow, offensive to his memory, criminal even.

But God never said life would make sense, did He? She would adjust. Just as she had when her mother had died. Whether she liked it or not, the sun kept coming up every morning and she was still breathing. Soon there would be another life for her to care for. Her focus should be there and she would get through this. Somehow.

Still, existing and adjusting weren't the same as really feeling peace and hope, and it seemed the more she reached at those things, the more the little voice inside told her she'd be alone. Always alone.

As usual, Becky avoided looking at the large portrait of Tommy hanging above the server. Instead, she studied the gardens on the other side of the terrace. Aggie moved on to a new section of her newspaper. The pendulum of an old grandfather clock ticked off the long seconds. Four more months of this? It wasn't going to be easy. But at least she had her new job. And despite the less than warm greeting she'd received from Katie Winters yesterday, Becky hoped she would make some teacher friends at the school. Many of them seemed to know Aggie. Maybe they could serve as the topic for a more neutral conversation?

"I met some of the other teachers at the middle school," she said. "A Mrs. Tarrington and Georgia Miles. They teach seventh grade. They both say hello to you and that they'll see you at the garden club next month."

Aggie perked up with great interest despite her efforts to feign boredom at the new topic. Again, she thrust aside the large section of newspaper. "I don't know why Georgia is still teaching school. She could have retired years ago. She's married to a dentist. She doesn't need to work. But Mrs. Tarrington, her husband is a professor at the university. She'll have to work forever. Poor thing."

"You know, Aggie, some like working. I do. I love children, especially at the middle school age. They're old enough to understand difficult concepts and yet still young enough that they listen. I feel like I can make a difference in their lives."

"Oh, Rebecca, save your preaching. I used to work myself. Before Jack left home, I was on every kind of committee you can imagine."

Becky resisted the urge to smile. Was this a real conversation they were having? Their very first that wasn't about Tommy or the baby?

"Who else is still working up there?" Aggie asked.

"I met Katie Winters. Katie teaches the same subject

that I do. It seems we'll be working on a play together. Her brother, too. He's building the set."

"Oh, dear. Now, there's a good-for-nothing family." Aggie snorted in a low voice.

"You know, Justin worked in the ER at the hospital the day his team took me in. They weren't going to admit me, but he offered to stay and help out with the nurses' strike."

"Where did you hear that?" Aggie scoffed. "Ridiculous. My husband donated a heart unit to that hospital years ago. They wouldn't make a Kirkpatrick wait. I'm sure Dr. Klein arranged your admission if there was ever any doubt."

"Well, that would be odd, seeing as Dr. Klein is the one who told me about what Justin Winters had done."

"He did?"

"Yes. I asked him how the medics were able to gain my admission even with the strike and he told me about Justin."

"Well, don't go thinking he's some sort of hero. I can't believe he's still allowed to work in any capacity in the medical field. It's a wonder he got you to the hospital alive. Listen to me, Rebecca, the Winters family is nothing but trouble. Ask anyone. They'll tell you the same. You stay away from them. It's what Tommy would have wanted."

What Tommy would have wanted? Why? What would Tommy have cared about her working on a play with another teacher, and getting help from a doctor? That seemed odd. About as odd as Katie and Justin's behavior to her at the school that day. Becky frowned, thinking there must be a story there somewhere. But what? Or did she really want to know?

Chapter Six

Becky wrote the weekend assignment on the board while her students whispered anxiously about the after-school try-outs for the play.

"Mrs. K, are you going to help direct the play?" one student shouted.

"Mrs. Fox always helped with the play," another said.

Other students agreed in unison that she should help with the play. Becky grinned as she replaced the chalk under the green board and walked back to her desk. It felt nice to be liked and wanted by the new students. They had no idea how much they helped her to get through each new day.

"What play?" she teased them.

"Mrs. K!" They all laughed at her feigned ignorance.

Becky laughed, too, but she wasn't exactly sure how to answer them. All week, she'd struggled over how to approach Katie Winters about working together on the sixth-grade play. While she didn't want to force her help on anyone, Becky couldn't allow others to do her work for her, especially if she was going to take credit for it at the final production. And she wasn't dense. After her conversation with Aggie about the Winters family and Katie and Justin's strange behavior toward her on her first day of work, Becky knew there was some bad history between the two families. And that was a shame. But she didn't see how it had anything to do with her and doing a job with middle school children. Bottom line was that Becky felt great on her new diet—no cramps, no fatigue. Also, she loved working with the children. She longed to be around other people with a task in hand and she loved the theater—she'd directed several plays in her former teaching position. In short, she wanted and needed to be a part of this.

Katie Winters, however, had made herself scarce all week. Although her classroom was right across the hall from Becky's, she seemed to be there only when the room was full of children, and Becky had not seen her once in the cafeteria at lunchtime. She hated to show up at the first practice without talking to Katie first, but if that's what she had to do, then that's what she had to do.

"So, class, since the play you're doing is a modern adaptation of *Cyrano de Bergerac,* tell me, what do you know about it?"

"It's really old," said a boy in the back row.

A child in the front raised a hand. "It was written by Edmond Rostand."

Becky nodded at their enthusiasm.

"It's French," shouted a small redheaded girl.

One student with a severe case of attention deficit jumped out of her chair. "My mom said that Cyrano was a real person. Is that true?"

Becky smiled and motioned for the girl to get back in her seat. "All of that is true. But what do you know about the characters? For example, about the character Cyrano?"

"He had a big nose," said a tall girl from the center of the room.

"Yeah, he was ugly," said the student next to her.

"He was goofy," added another, wanting in on the criticisms.

The one child in the front row raised her hand again. "He liked poetry."

"Yes, he did. And was good at it. And was a good swordsman, although in our story he's a basketball player. The best on the team," Becky explained. "He was a master of many things—what we would call a larger-than-life character. Can anyone expand on that?"

The class fell silent. Finally one student raised his hand—a tall, quiet boy in the back.

"William?" Becky pointed to him.

"Cyrano was a Renaissance man and a good friend. And a hero because of his genius. But he wasn't attractive."

All the students turned to William with their mouths hanging open. Even the know-it-all from the front row. William was new to the school and it was the first time since she'd been there that he'd spoken. He was a handsome child, with a pleasant expression and an easygoing manner.

Becky nodded at his comment. "Right, he wasn't attractive. And that made him a bit of a twist on the typical romantic hero."

"This is a love story?" one boy asked in a tone that sounded as if he'd just tasted something disgusting. He finished his question by pretending to die of strangulation in the center aisle.

The girls giggled. The boys booed.

"Yes, Cyrano is a love story...." Becky glared down at the child. "Let's save the acting for the stage."

She allowed them a minute to settle and the child to get back into his seat, then continued. "But it's also a story of friendships and sacrifice."

A knock sounded at her classroom door before she could go on.

"Okay, class, why don't you all start on your homework and work until the bell rings? That will give you five minutes less work to do at home tonight."

With a few moans, the students opened their reading books. Although a few went back to whispering about the play tryouts—it seemed all the girls wanted to be Roxane and all the boys wanted to play the handsome Christian.

Becky walked to the door. Mr. Combes, the school principal, stood there, his lips furled into a deep grimace as he surveyed the classroom.

"I'm afraid I have some bad news," he said.

Becky's heart raced. Bad news? Was her boss already unhappy with her work? She hoped not. But what else could he have come to say?

Becky stepped out of the room and into the hallway as Mr. Combes had motioned for her to do. She looked back at the class and pulled the door shut. "They're not usually this rowdy, sir. They're just very excited about the play tryouts this afternoon."

"Well, that's what I came to talk to you about. Ms. Winters is out sick today—bad case of the flu. She's not going to be able to help you this afternoon with the tryouts."

"Oh." Becky sucked in a quick breath to keep from smiling. She wasn't happy that Katie was ill. She was, however, pretty relieved this visit from the principal didn't have to do with her own teaching. "Well, I'm sorry she's sick. But don't worry about the tryouts. I'll be fine."

"Really?" Mr. Combes's face started to relax into a smile. "Outside the classroom, they can be a bit difficult."

"I'll be fine. I've been looking forward to getting started on this project all week. It's going to be great."

"Well, thank you," he said, already huffing his way off down the hallway, checking his cell phone. "You're a lifesaver."

* * *

An hour later Becky stood at the front of the stage in the school auditorium with a clipboard in hand. "Thank you all for trying out. Everyone did a fabulous job, but as you know there are only fourteen speaking roles, so not everyone will have a major part. If you are interested in working on props or costumes—"

The back door to the stage flew open, letting in streams of bright afternoon sunlight. Justin Winters's large silhouette stepped into the door frame.

"Major Winters!" the students all shouted as if a rock star had suddenly graced their presence.

"I've got a truck full of building materials for a certain play I hear is going to take place soon. Any chance I could get some help unloading it?" Although Justin blocked most of the light coming through the stage door, Becky could still see the boyish smile on his face as he dipped his head and glanced over at her. Now, *that* was the smile she'd seen in the coffee shop—the one that could turn women into slushies. "Can you spare a few men to help me, Teach?"

Becky felt a little warmth creeping up her neck as Justin looked over. She hadn't expected to see him. And after their last meeting she certainly hadn't expected him to be so friendly. Maybe the awkwardness had all been because of Katie. But why?

Becky also didn't know how good a man could look in a pair of jeans and a polo shirt. Too good, with his hands on his slender hips and his big brown puppy-dog eyes cutting at her. But good grief, why was he delivering the building supplies during the tryouts? Talk about disruptive. She looked away quickly, hoping her expression didn't reveal her pleasure in seeing him.

"Major Winters! I can help!" A large number of boys raised hands and hollered. "I'll help the doctor!"

The girls, too, went wide-eyed and moved with excitement at the prospect. "We can help, too," a few of them called out.

"Settle down, boys and girls." Becky looked over the group. They settled back in their seats quickly and became quiet.

"Impressive." Justin's cheeks flushed with red as he dropped his hands and ambled closer to her. "Like a true commander."

"Doesn't take the army to make kids behave. Even with such a big interruption," she teased. "I didn't know you were so popular."

"Sorry about that. Katie has the students write to my unit once a month. So they feel like they know me."

"That's nice. A great idea, actually." Becky sucked in a quick breath to keep up with her ever-increasing heartbeat. "Anyway, we're almost finished. I just need to see six students for a second reading." She called out her short list. "The rest of you are dismissed unless Doctor Winters needs your help." She gestured to Justin.

Once again, the students became excited. But when Justin stepped to the edge of the stage and surveyed them, the effect of his commanding stance was immediate. Chatter ceased and everyone sat attentively in his or her seat, waiting for him to pick a few good men, or boys in this case. Becky smiled inwardly, thinking that Katie had probably solicited Justin's help on the play for more than simply his expertise in building sets.

But why was he here today? Becky wondered if Katie had sent Justin to check on her. The building supplies could have been dropped off at another time. It wasn't like they were going to start building anything today. Becky also wondered how Katie would feel about the fact that she had done quite well, all alone with the students.

Becky set her attention on the six students in front of her, ready to work on new parts. She turned the script to the most challenging scene. If Dr. Winters had come to see if she could handle herself with the kids, then why not show him just how well she could do it?

Justin felt a little silly showing up at the school unneeded and unannounced. It was obvious he'd surprised Becky and disrupted a smooth-running tryout. He hadn't wanted to come over at all, but his sister—stuck home with a rotten case of the flu—had insisted that he check on Becky and see how she was handling the tryouts. What he was really doing, now that he thought about it, was spying on her and he could hardly believe he'd agreed to it. Now all he wanted to do was to unload the truck and get out of there as fast as possible.

He looked out over the group of students. Most of the boys had seated themselves together in the back. He chose four of the boys with raised hands. The group followed him to the parking lot directly behind the stage. Justin gave them some instructions and they began unloading the building supplies from the back of the truck. He picked the tallest one to work with him.

"What's your name?"

"William."

The boy had dark features—hair, eyes and skin. Justin guessed he might be of Native American descent. And although a bit clumsy, he would probably turn out to be a large and powerful man.

They carried in the long segments of heavy pressboard, cans of paint and other materials, working quickly. Justin was glad. If they continued at this pace, he wouldn't be there more than five minutes. That was a relief since he shouldn't have been there at all.

Although he was not sorry to see Becky again. He would keep his distance from her for everyone's sake, but the truth was he liked Becky Kirkpatrick and liked her company. He was glad to see her looking well and having fun with the students. He could only imagine how hard the last few months of her life had been.

On the stage, she worked with the six students she'd called. He could hear them reading aloud the lines to the play. Occasionally, she would stop them, make some comments, then they'd reread the portion of script. Katie would have been pleased. Actually, Katie would have been amazed. Becky had a natural way with the students, which was both engaging and authoritative. And if she had looked tired when he'd seen her earlier in the week, she'd gotten over it, because this afternoon she appeared positively radiant. He'd always heard pregnant women could glow. And Becky Kirkpatrick was glowing, much like she'd been that morning at the coffee shop when he'd met her.

Justin had to hand it to Tommy. His former friend had found and married one of the most beautiful women Justin had ever laid eyes on.

Then left her.

Justin thought of Gentry, dying in his arms. Had Tommy died in Becky's? Probably. He could barely imagine how horrible that must have been for them both.

"She's the prettiest teacher I've ever had. And really smart, too."

Justin pulled his gaze away from Becky and focused on the youth helping him carry in the large squares of pressboard. But what was he supposed to say to that? "Well, teachers should be smart, shouldn't they?"

The kid nodded, looking a little embarrassed about his words.

"Did you try out for the play?" Justin asked him.

"Sure." The kid's moss-colored eyes glanced down at the boards they carried to the back of the stage.

"Which role?"

"Cyrano."

"Right." Justin laughed. "I guess all the guys tried out for Cyrano."

"Actually, no. They all tried out for Christian."

Justin lifted his eyebrow suspiciously. "Really? But he's not the hero."

"I guess he seems cooler than Cyrano to some people."

Justin let his comment sink in for a moment while he adjusted the large planks over a precariously placed set of stairs. "But not to you?"

The boy shrugged as they turned to go back out to the truck.

"Hey, William," Becky called from the other side of the stage. "Could I get you to read one more scene, please?"

"Sure, Mrs. K.," William answered eagerly. And looking over at Becky, he missed the top step leading up to the back stage. The boy fell hard, knocking over the boards they'd set down. His body thudded down the dark set of stairs. The back of his head hit hard against the wood railing. Then the pile of lumber slid down over his legs.

"William!" Becky gasped. Throwing her notes to the ground, she hurried over. The other students on the stage moved in close, too. Some of them giggled, others whispered, some turned away.

"Back away. Give him some space." Justin shooed the other children away from the scene. He lifted the lumber carefully and placed it far out of the way of the stairs. The students crowded back around William. "Let me through so I can help him, kids."

The cluster of children parted and Justin hurried down next to the boy. William moaned and tried to press up.

"Hold on, William." Justin checked his pupils. "How's your head?"

"It's fine. I can get up." A faint wheeze sounded in his breath.

Justin checked his leg. It didn't appear to be broken. "You want to try and stand up?"

The boy nodded, his breathing becoming more and more stressed, with short quick intakes.

"Relax, William. Slow down your breathing." Justin put an arm under the boy's shoulders for support. "Let's try to stand."

Slowly, they lifted up together. He hoped moving him would relax the child a bit, but Justin doubted it. He seemed nearly panic-stricken. And as soon as William put weight on his left foot, he collapsed completely into Justin's support and his wheezing increased. Almost a whistle now.

"Sit back down. Let me look at your leg again." Justin helped William sit back on the last step then crouched down in front of him. "Do you often have this much trouble breathing?"

William shook his head. "I—I…"

"Never mind. Don't speak," Justin said. "You're not getting enough air to breathe much less to try and talk."

Justin looked around for Becky. Maybe she knew something about this child's asthma.

"Slow your breathing if you can. Think long and deep." Justin rolled up the boy's jeans and examined William's leg. It wasn't broken. But probably he had a bad sprain that would keep him off his feet for a bit and cause some nice swelling. "No worries. It's not broken. But you might have sprained it. You should stay off it until we can get an X-ray. Right now, I'm more concerned about your breathing. You have asthma, don't you?"

William nodded, his eyes large as he sucked in more

short, quick and ineffective breaths. It was similar to what had happened to Becky at the hospital, although hers had been caused by the gestational diabetes, and had been manageable with the oxygen they'd administered. But this child had real asthma and without something to open up his bronchial passages in the next few minutes, he was going to asphyxiate.

"That's okay. That's okay. Do you have an inhaler?"

William nodded and pointed to his back.

"How's he doing?" Becky asked, approaching him now that all the students had moved off the stage and settled into their seats.

"He needs his inhaler. Must be in his backpack."

William nodded.

"I'll get it." Becky raced off, asking students to pass up William's schoolbag. Her hands were already digging inside of it when she returned to the staircase. She located the inhaler kit and handed it to Justin.

Justin snapped the medicine vial into the dispenser and held it up to William's mouth. "One, two, three."

He administered the medicine. Relief showed in William's face as his air passageways reopened, allowing in the precious oxygen he so desperately needed.

"How do you feel, William?"

"Better," he whispered.

"Good." He turned to Becky. "Do you or the school know anything about his condition?"

"I didn't." Becky waved a student over. "I'll send Callie to fetch Mr. Combes and William's parents."

"No. No. No." William's eyes bulged and he tried to stand. "Don't—don't tell my mom. She—she…"

"She what?" Justin pushed William back down on the step.

"Well…" William looked down at the floor. "She just gets really upset about stuff."

"About your asthma?"

"Right."

Becky lifted an eyebrow. "We have to tell your parents, William. And the school."

"Fine. Then scratch me off the play. I won't be able to be in it."

Justin glanced sideways at Becky. Sounded like some trouble brewing at home for this kid.

"Let's worry about one thing at a time, shall we?" Becky moved off to get the principal and deal with the other students.

Keeping one hand on William's shoulder, Justin sat next to the boy. "How are we doing, buddy? I know it hurts."

The boy looked pale. He moistened his lips. "I'm totally fine. I just wish you guys wouldn't call my mom."

"I know. But we have to," he said. "Now, I'm going to get your leg up and wrap it a little in ice. It might hurt some but it's what we need to do, so that it will heal faster. Okay?"

William nodded.

Justin asked a student to fetch him ice and a wrap from the school clinic. Then he returned to William. "Now why don't you tell me about your asthma while we wait for your parents and the principal?"

"There's nothing to tell," William said. "I've had it forever. Chronic. Mostly stress induced."

Becky returned, as did the girl Justin had sent to the clinic, with ice and a long ACE bandage. "Principal Combes is getting William's mom. I'm dismissing the other students."

Justin carefully wrapped William's foot and ankle. Becky returned to them about the time he was finished.

"Wow. Look at that wrap, William." She tousled the dark

curls on the top of William's head—a soft, motherly gesture. Protective, loving, concerned—Becky might have the name Kirkpatrick but she wore it with her own signature. "Good thing Dr. Winters was here. Nothing like having your own private flight surgeon. I wonder if we're going to have a Cyrano on crutches?"

William let a slow smile creep over his face as well as bright red blush.

Justin swallowed hard, not liking Becky's praise since he felt the accident was completely his fault. If he hadn't listened to Katie, he wouldn't have been at the school and this would have never happened. He shouldn't have come to the tryouts. Becky had been fine on her own. Now she had a student—apparently the star student—with a sprained ankle. William also had a crush on her. That made two of them.

Justin was not sorry when Becky turned away to meet the principal and the boy's mother, who had entered the far end of the auditorium together. The mother had the same dark features as her son, except that she was petite. And she was shaking with worry by the time Becky had finished talking to her. He hoped that William had been wrong about suspecting his mother to be against his participating in the play, but the conversation wasn't looking too positive.

Becky looked worn down, much more so than when he'd first arrived. And he knew that was his fault. He'd caused problems by having come to the tryouts—sent a kid into respiratory arrest, let him fall down and sprain his ankle, caused the teacher extra worry, time and frustration.

He looked at her, so concerned about the mother's reaction that she was close to tears of exhaustion. Justin was moved. Becky may have been married to Tommy, who was a jerk, but she clearly was a lovely lady. And he hadn't been honest with her. It was starting to eat away at his conscience. Maybe, it was time to start things over with Becky.

But would he make things better by telling her the truth, or would he just make things worse?

Chapter Seven

"Well, that was an exciting first day." Becky took a deep breath and fell exhausted into the director's chair at the edge of the stage. "I hope that's not an indication of things to come."

Justin gave her comment a businesslike nod of acknowledgement as he finished unloading the rest of the building materials and locked up the stage doors. Becky watched him from her chair, suddenly realizing the two of them were alone.

"So, why did you bring the supplies today? I noticed on the schedule they weren't expected for delivery until next week." She tried to sound more curious than suspicious.

Justin walked over, narrowing his eyes on her. He studied her. And his intense gaze was unnerving. Heat rose to her cheeks and she lifted a hand to her face to hide from his scrutiny.

And her own embarrassment. She shouldn't have asked the question about why he'd come. It sounded as if she were fishing. Like she hoped he'd say he came to see *her.* "I guess the supplies were just ready to deliver, huh?"

He didn't reply, other than to stop beside her chair and lean one shoulder against the wall, continuing to study her face. A hint of his cologne wafted over her, setting her senses on high alert and her tired brain on the defense. "I should have known about William's condition. I wonder why his mother hasn't informed the school about his asthma?"

Finally, Justin's intensity waned. He crossed his arms over his chest and let out a long, deep sigh. "It's hard to know why people neglect something as important as that. She seemed really shaken up."

"I noticed that, too. But she didn't say anything to me or to the principal. She just listened and said she'd get him to a doctor. I hope this doesn't cause problems for him. He seems like such a nice kid. I'll be really disappointed if he can't participate in the play. He's very talented."

Justin nodded. Turning back to her, he placed a hand on her shoulder. Her eyes lifted. "You look pale, Becky. Have you checked your blood sugar lately?"

She hadn't. In all the excitement, she'd forgotten, which was probably why she felt so tired. But she didn't feel like sharing that with Justin. He'd done enough. And she didn't like that he hadn't answered her question about bringing the supplies early. It made her think even more about the conversation with Aggie warning her away from the Winters family. Now, it was her turn not to answer. A wave of dizziness blurred Becky's vision. She dropped her head, closed her eyes and pressed her hand against her temple.

Justin crouched beside her. "Yep. That's what I thought. Do you have a meter?"

She nodded without looking up at him. "It's in my bag. Over there."

Justin retrieved the device from her bag and readied it without speaking.

"Will William be okay?" she asked, wanting the focus off herself.

"Yes. He'll be fine." Justin pulled her arm to him and

tested her. She didn't even feel the prick. "Low. You have something to eat? Some orange juice?"

"No. But I'll get something at home."

"No. You should eat something right now. Wait here. I'll be right back." He handed the meter to her then darted off down one of the auditorium aisles.

Becky forced herself out of the chair, fighting the dizziness and blurred vision. It was getting late. Aggie would start worrying. She grabbed her bag and headed for the doors.

Justin blocked her exit. "What are you doing? You're going to pass out again, Becky. You've got to take gestational diabetes seriously."

"I know. It's just that it's late and…" He was right. She had to stay on top of this or she wouldn't be able to keep the job. And she needed the job. "You're right. I need to eat."

"That's better. Here. Sit. Eat." Justin handed her a granola bar and pointed to the first row of seats.

She took the snack from his hand. "Where did you get this?"

"Vending. There's a machine down the hall. Now sit down. And eat."

"I'm not in the army, you know."

Another stern look and Becky did as he said, her body feeling better the minute the sugars from the snack hit her bloodstream.

He sat down beside her, his body tense and restless. His long legs shifted from one position to the next. All that awkwardness from the last time she'd seen him filled the room. Again, Becky thought of Aggie's warning and was angry for not having watched her blood sugar. If she had, she could have already been home. She wondered how long he was going to make her sit there before she could escape.

"You asked me a question a few minutes ago and I didn't

answer," he started, ending the long silence that passed while she chewed.

She glanced over. "It's no big deal. I just wasn't expecting you, but—"

"I know. And you were thinking if I hadn't come, William wouldn't have gotten hurt. I was thinking the exact same thing."

Becky pressed her lips together and looked away. That wasn't exactly what she'd been thinking. More like that he and Katie had plotted to see if she could handle the job.

"I feel awful about it," he continued. "I shouldn't have brought the supplies. And the truth is I hadn't planned on it, but I got off work early and Katie was home sick and all worried that you needed help. She asked me to check on you. So, I brought the supplies early and… I'm really sorry."

"So, do you feel bad about William hurting his leg and having an asthma attack or do you feel bad about spying on me?"

Justin finally raised his head and looked her in the eye, his expression full of regret. "I feel bad about both. I'm sorry. Katie can be difficult sometimes but I should have refused to do it."

"Well, I'm the one that called William over and distracted him. I had a hand in it, too. So, what will you tell your sister?"

Justin let a grin play at his lips. "That she needs your help with the play. You were great. I was listening to the six kids you were working with on the stage and I couldn't believe those were sixth graders. They sounded as if they really understood the lines."

"They do really understand the lines." Becky let out a quick laugh. "And frankly, I'd appreciate your help with Katie. She seems reluctant about me working on the play but I don't shirk duty so she's getting my help whether she wants it or not. I'd prefer it if she'd welcome it."

"I owe you that after turning this afternoon into such a fiasco. But…" His face winced as if he were in pain. Whatever he had to say, he did not want to say it.

Becky lifted her bag to her shoulder and stood to leave. This day had been long enough. Anything that could make a man look that distressed, she did not want to talk about today. "Thanks for the food. I feel much better now. And you're right. I will be one hundred percent diligent about testing and my six little meals a day, no matter what schedule changes I have. I do not want to end up back in that hospital before it's time."

Becky was halfway down the aisle when she heard Justin rise and move after her. "But, Becky, wait… One more thing. Please, can you give me a second?"

One more thing? That thing that made you cringe? Uh… No, thank you. *The Winters family is nothing but trouble.* Aggie's words played through her head. She marched on though the doors and into the hallway, barely glancing back over her shoulder. It surprised her to see that he had stood and followed her. "Look, Justin. I'm tired. How about another time? I'll see you next week at play practice… And thanks for talking to your sister. I do appreciate it."

"Sure, Becky, but…" He stepped up behind her, slowing his pace as he caught up. His steady gaze on the back of her head and then his hand on her shoulder felt warm and gentle. "I need to say this. Please. Please, give me a minute. This isn't easy."

Releasing a frustrated sigh, Becky turned to face him. His chocolate eyes fell soft and pleading to her face, melting the tiny bit of resolve left inside her.

"I—I didn't know who you were when we met in the

coffee shop last week." His jaw tensed, the muscles in his face flexing.

Becky swallowed. Hard. "Who I was? What do you mean? You know me?"

"No." He closed his eyes. "I knew…."

Tommy. He knew Tommy. Becky's heart pounded so hard she could hear it. Her hands balled into fists. So, the bad family connection had to do with Tommy and Justin. She should have seen that coming. They had to be the same age or close to it. It was a small town. Of course they knew each other. So, now Justin was going to speak about her husband. Well, she didn't want him to. She was tired, emotional, ready to cry. And if it was something bad he had to say about Tommy then he could just keep that to himself. Whatever it was Justin had to say, she did not want to hear it. Not ever.

"Don't." She held up a hand to silence him. "Your condolences aren't needed. There's a point where you have to move on and I've reached that. So thank you. But it's—"

"I do need to say this. And I need to tell you who I am. I would have said it sooner but no one told me about his—"

"Really, it's okay. I understand. You just got home from Afghanistan." Becky trembled, her hands, her legs, her lips. Her head shook back and forth. She did not want to speak about Tommy. Not with Justin.

"No, you *don't* understand." Justin tightened his grip on her shoulder. "I didn't just know Tommy. He and I used to be friends. Good friends… Best friends."

Becky frowned. She had known Tommy's friends. All of them. Justin had never been mentioned. With her hand, she pressed Justin's arm away from her shoulder. "He never mentioned you. Why are you saying this? It can't be true. I knew all of Tommy's friends."

"We—we lost touch. I didn't even know he'd married. And since I came home from active duty, no one had a chance to tell me about his passing. Anyway, Becky, the point is that Tommy was a huge part of my life at one point—almost like a brother. This is a small town and you were bound to find that out at some point, since Tommy never mentioned me to you. I wanted you to hear it from me."

"You wanted me to hear what from you?" Becky shook her head back and forth. "What is it that I'm going to find out? That you were friends? You couldn't have been close. Tommy would have mentioned someone so close to him."

"Come on, Becky. Why would I make this up? What could I possibly have to gain?"

"I can't imagine." She put a hand to her head. This conversation was making it ache. "So, explain to me what happened. Why would I not have heard of you?"

Justin stood there, silent as a mute with his irksome brown eyes so full of compassion and concern Becky nearly had to turn away.

"You're making it sound like Tommy wasn't truthful with me." True anger laced words. She dropped her head; it was throbbing now. "Then again, even Aggie…" She paused, looked up at him and shook her head again. "You know? Never mind. I'm leaving."

"What did Aggie tell you?" Justin took hold of her wrist. His fingers were warm and she could feel his pulse beating against her skin. Tears threatened the corners of her eyes.

"Nothing." Becky pressed her lips together and looked down at the floor. "Just that I should stay away from you and your sister. Now, why would she say that?"

Justin sighed and his hand fell away. He looked hard into her eyes and she could see the tendons in his jaw flexing. It seemed Justin struggled as much as she did to maintain composure. Little beads of sweat had formed on his brow. "I can't, Becky. I'm sorry I brought it up. It's not my place."

"You said you wanted me to hear it from you…"

Justin shook his head. "Well, maybe I was wrong. I didn't mean to upset you. Just thought I should tell you that I knew Tommy. That's all."

Right. There was a whole lot more to this story and sooner or later she'd find out. Wouldn't she? Anger rose in her. She backed up a step, putting some distance between them. "At least tell me how you and Tommy were such good friends?"

With the back of his hand, Justin wiped his face with a quick, awkward movement. "Our fathers worked together. Actually, my father worked for Tommy's father…"

"And?"

"And in summers, my dad would drive me to the Kirkpatricks' place almost every day. We were in school together. Scouts. Football. Everything…"

"Impossible." Becky turned away. Tommy had never mentioned Justin. Not even once. "I don't believe you. I would have heard about you…."

"I'm sorry I've upset you." He touched her shoulder again. He looked truly pained over the conversation. "You're right. It was a long time ago. Hardly worth mentioning. I'm sorry."

And with a few giant steps, he'd fled the auditorium, leaving Becky alone with a face full of tears.

Chapter Eight

Becky could scarcely believe it. Aggie had come to church.
There hadn't even been a discussion or a reminder, not even
a moment's hesitation. In fact, at ten-thirty sharp, Mrs. Fitzwilliams had picked them both up from Greyfield and there
they now sat in the third row of Glendale First Community
Church for the eleven o'clock service.

Despite the old stained-glass windows and traditional
wooden pews, the service was much less formal than Becky
had anticipated. The minister was young and the congregation formed primarily of growing families. The choir sang
some of her favorites. Becky reveled in the music and the
words of thanks and praise. It had been far too long since
she'd been to worship. She'd been afraid church would
remind her of Tommy's funeral and make her sad. Instead,
it filled her heart with joy and gave her that sense of peace
she'd longed for.

Aggie didn't sing. Nor did she read the memory verse
along with the congregation. But she didn't scowl or make
other condescending faces and when the offering plate came
by she wrote a generous check and tossed it into the basket.
This was not her first time in a church. And judging by
the number of people rushing over to visit Aggie after the

service, Becky guessed it wasn't her first time in this church, either. Many people lavished her with compliments and invitations to lunch. Some sounded more sincere than others, but it was clear that Aggie Kirkpatrick was both respected and welcomed in this place. So why did she pretend to have such a dislike for it?

Becky, too, saw many faces she knew: Dr. Klein, a few teachers from the middle school, Katie and Justin and several students, including William who tore past her on a pair of metal crutches. Immediately, Becky looked across the sanctuary for his mother. This would be a good time to make sure she was okay with all that had happened at the practice on Friday.

"Justin said that the tryouts went well."

Becky recognized Katie Winters's voice even with its added nasal quality, probably due to her bout with the flu. Becky turned slowly to face her. Katie wasn't smiling, but she didn't look as tense as she had the first time they'd met. Becky had hoped to avoid both Katie and her brother, at least until she'd had a chance to talk to Aggie about Tommy and Justin. She wasn't at all sure what to make of her strange conversation with Justin after the practice on Friday. Last night, after Aggie had gone to sleep, she'd spent two hours looking through old Kirkpatrick photo albums. There was not one picture of Justin Winters in any of them. What was she supposed to make of that? How could she believe any of what Justin had told her? And yet something deep inside made her feel that Justin was telling the truth. And how upsetting to even consider that Tommy had kept a secret from her—poor, dear Tommy. If he'd kept something from her, then he must have had a reason.

She swallowed hard and forced a pleasant smile. "Yes, it went well. If you're feeling up to it, we could discuss my recommendations for the different roles. I think you'll be pleased."

Katie straightened her short, dark bob, pressing strands from both sides behind her ears, her face expressionless. "Right. Actually... I only came over to say thanks for filling in while I was sick on Friday. I'll read over the recommendations—I'm sure they're good. But if you don't mind, I'll have the students read again tomorrow after school and that way I can have some input, as well."

She was saying *thank you but I'll take over from here.* Becky started to protest but stopped as a wild sensation rolled through her belly.

"Are you okay?" Katie asked, actually looking concerned.

"I think so— I just—" And then it happened again. A flutter. Maybe more like a flip. Yes, that was it. Something inside her had flipped. That couldn't be good, could it? Becky filled with a mixture of joy and fear.

Katie frowned at her. "Well, you don't *have* to work on the play with me—"

"Oh, no, no." Becky waved her hands in the air. "Of course I want to work on the play. Your idea sounds—"

"Hi, Ms. Winters. Mrs. K." William Gaines popped up between them on his new metal crutches.

"Hello, William. How's the ankle?" Becky asked. "This is the brave young man who fell at the tryouts on Friday afternoon."

"It wasn't a big deal." William shrugged.

"Well, it was kind of a big deal. You're on crutches," Becky corrected.

William shrugged. "Glad Major Winters was there. He knew how to give me my medicine."

Katie nodded, smiling at the mention of her brother. "I heard about that."

Becky pressed into her side where she'd felt the fluttering of motion. She wanted to feel it again. Or did she? "You know, William was also the only student to try out for the role of Cyrano. And he did a very nice job. You'll get to see for yourself tomorrow."

William dropped his arms and his head. "Actually, that's why I came over. I'm not going to be in the play," he said with a long face.

Becky frowned. "But why? You seemed so excited about it. You tried out for the lead."

William glanced over his shoulder at his mother who was motioning that it was time to leave. "It's just not going to work out this year."

"William, is this because of what happened on Friday?"

He shrugged. "Not really."

"Well, think about it some more. We're extending the try-outs another day."

"Okay." William turned away and moved toward his mother.

"That's disappointing. Maybe he'll change his mind," Becky said.

"Yes." Katie sighed before returning to their interrupted conversation. "Are you sure with your health issues that you can handle the play?"

Health issues? Exactly what had Justin said to his sister? "I'm fine, I assure you. I wouldn't be working at the school at all if it was a risk."

She probably should have smiled, but she didn't. She was truly disappointed at Katie's resistance and William's decision.

And once again the strange flutter rippled through her belly. It was startling. But not painful. She wasn't sure if she should be concerned or excited about it. In either case, she wanted to get away from Katie so she could decide. Not to mention, Aggie was waiting. Becky stepped away. "See you tomorrow."

Katie made a quirky face and walked away.

Fine. Becky was over it. She wasn't thrilled with the idea of working together, either. Becky spun away fast. But she didn't get far. Justin placed a stiff arm at her shoulder to keep her from plowing into his chest. Great. Not that she minded he was at the church, but she needed more time after their last conversation. Time to accept or deny what he'd told her. She didn't see how it could be true.

Justin greeted her with apprehension. And again the strange sensation undulated across her belly. Becky was wide-eyed but smiling this time. Was it what she thought it was? Could it be?

"You okay?" Justin asked.

"Fine." She backed away a step. "Just need to get going."

"Oh, well. I only came over to—"

"You don't have to bring up the other day," she interrupted. "It's fine. I don't need to know all of—"

"No. No." He stopped her, spreading that charming grin of his and melting her with those warm, chocolate eyes. "I was going to welcome you to our church."

"Oh." *Oops.* Her cheeks grew warm. "Thank you."

Justin looked down with apologetic eyes. "Also, I didn't get a chance to talk to Katie about your continuing to work on the play. She was pretty sick. I was surprised she came to church this morning."

Becky lifted her chin, taking in Justin's army dress blues. Twenty or so colorful medals and pins at his breast caught her eye. Like the man needed something else to draw attention to his six-foot-four frame. He was indeed a handsome man. Next to his height and broad shoulders, Becky felt petite. She liked that she had to tilt her head up to look into his eyes. "You didn't talk to her? She seemed to know about my health."

"I think you told her that you'd been in the hospital. And I did mention that you'd held a great tryout, but that was all. Like I said, she was pretty ill."

Oops, again.

A group of people walked by and patted Justin on the shoulder welcoming him home. She looked away and took a deep breath. She needed to relax and get off the defensive. The past was the past. If there even was a past.

She needed to think about the good things in her future, like Aggie coming to church, the kids at school and the play, and—

It came again—that rippling twist of movement through her core. Could it be? Could she be feeling her baby move for the first time? The idea flooded her with excitement. This time she smiled and put her hand on her belly where she'd last felt the new sensation. She wanted the movement to come again. So she could be sure.

Justin was glad for the interruption from Mr. Elfkin and Pastor Dean. He'd gotten too caught up in talking to Becky. People were sure to notice, and wonder. Like Matt had said, everyone knew there was bad blood between the Kirkpatrick and Winters families. He hadn't meant to talk to her long enough to draw attention, though he *had* come over to apologize for upsetting her on Friday. Actually, he'd come over to welcome her to church as he said, but he had also felt bad about bringing up a subject that had upset her so much, especially after a difficult afternoon.

Justin felt torn. Every time he looked at Becky, it was like someone was ripping him in half. He liked Becky. Despite all logic and pride and reason, he liked Becky Kirkpatrick.

She was sweet and smart and beautiful and he wanted to know her better. At the same time, there was all this past between them—a past she didn't even know about. He wanted to tell her the truth. Then, maybe they could be friends. But on Friday, once he'd started to talk, he'd realized that he couldn't do it. He couldn't tell Becky about what Tommy had done to Katie. It would hurt her. That is, if she even believed him. And if she didn't, then the two of them could never even be friends.

Becky made a strange face. Again. This was at least the third time over the course of the short conversation. And now she grabbed at her midsection. The doctor in him wanted an explanation. "You're sure you're okay? You're not cramping? Having pain?"

She shot him a look.

"You made a face," he explained. "And I am a doctor."

"I'm fine."

"So, should I still speak to Katie? When I came over, it sounded as if maybe you'd already worked it out."

"Yes, maybe we have."

"Good. I saw William, too."

"Yes." She looked down with disappointment. "I hate that he doesn't want to be in the production. He would have made a good Cyrano, even with his bad ankle."

"I hope that didn't have anything to do with his accident and the asthma." Justin moistened his dry lips.

"Me, too. Maybe I should talk to his mom?"

"He didn't seem too keen on that idea the other day." Justin pressed his lips together and shifted his weight. He folded and refolded the beret in his hands.

"True. In any case, your sister wants to hear the kids read again tomorrow so who knows? Maybe another Cyrano will emerge."

So, things hadn't gone that smoothly with his sister, if

Katie was holding the tryouts again. Becky was being a good sport about it. Maybe he'd talk to Katie anyway. "You know my sister is sometimes slow to warm up to people, but she's a good person. You'll see. And I think— I think…" *I think you're very pretty. And Tommy was a mighty lucky man.* "I think you'll enjoy working on the play."

"Thanks, Justin. I'm sure I will." Again, Becky's eyes went wide. And this time she gasped.

"That's it. Tell me what is happening. Do you need to sit down? Are you having pain?" A wave of panic flooded through Justin. He was going to get this woman to take care of herself and her baby whether she liked it or not. He reached his hands to her shoulders and lowered his head to her eye level, checking her pupils.

Becky pushed his hands away with a light touch and a laugh. "No. I thought it was a cramp, or something, but it isn't." Her voice was breathy with excitement. She moved her hand a little to the left then let out another laugh.

"You're okay? Are you sure?"

"I'm fine." She smiled. "The baby just kicked me… There! She did it again."

"Really." He stepped back, feeling a bit like an intruder in a private moment to which he did not belong. At the same time, a new emotion fell over him—a feeling of warmth and happiness and connection to the look of pure joy on Becky's face. Was this what it would feel like to be an expecting father? Worried. Excited. Amazed.

"This is so exciting. It's the first time. And so perfect that it happened today." She shook her head back and forth in delight. Then, in all her excitement, she leaned up and gave him a kiss on the cheek. A wave of heat shot from the spot on his cheek straight through Justin.

"I knew something wonderful would happen when Aggie

came to church... Actually, she's waiting for me. I have to go. See you at school."

"Right. Bye." Justin turned and watched her glide out of the sanctuary on her cloud of glee. He touched his hand to his face where she'd kissed him, knowing he felt entirely too much from the gesture. After a long moment, he let out a deep sigh and moved across the room toward his sister and mother.

Mrs. Fitzwilliams pulled in front of the Kirkpatricks' home. Becky and Aggie stepped out.

"I'll see you at bridge on Thursday," Mrs. Fitzwilliams said. "And plan on me picking up the two of you next Sunday morning. Same time."

Aggie turned back to her friend with a doubtful look.

"I won't take no for an answer," Mrs. Fitzwilliams said.

Aggie sighed. "I was going to offer to drive, Phyllis. That's all. But if you're going to be all cranky about it."

Becky leaned back into the car and mouthed a thank you to Aggie's friend. "Have a nice afternoon, Mrs. Fitzwilliams."

"Phyllis, dear. Call me Phyllis. And you keep taking care of that baby." She waved and sped down the drive like a blind NASCAR driver.

Phyllis was not a good driver. But if putting up with a little motion sickness was the price she paid for Aggie's attending church, she'd suffer it over and over. How happy this day would have made Tommy. She followed Aggie up the front stairs and into the house.

"Well?" Aggie said as soon as they stepped over the threshold. "You should just go ahead and tell me."

"What?" Had Aggie asked her something she'd forgotten to answer? "Are we still talking about the baby kicking?"

"No, Rebecca, I'm curious about your conversation with

the young Ms. Winters. I know you must want to make friends in Glendale, but you're not going to find one in that family."

"I see that, Aggie. Trust me. I don't think there's any chance of my becoming friends with Katie Winters. She had a comment to make about a project that we have to work on together at the school. That's all."

Aggie lifted an eyebrow. "I see. And Dr. Winters? You talked with him as well, did you not?"

"I did. He welcomed me to the church."

"I see."

I see. That was Aggie code for *I'm not satisfied with your answer.* But Becky wasn't in the mood to explain. In fact, she felt it was time someone told her why things were so touchy between the Winters family and the Kirkpatricks. It was starting to feel as if she was in a bad episode of *Dallas.*

"You know, Aggie, her brother, Justin, passed on his condolences the other day and mentioned that he and Tommy used to be close. I think he even said that they were like brothers. You said there were differences between the families. You didn't say anything about Tommy and Justin being friends."

Aggie's expression darkened. She turned away and called for the housekeeper. "Dyanna?"

Becky stepped after her. "No. Wait a minute, Aggie. This is important. It's clear that Katie feels awkward working with me at the school and is only doing so because she has no choice. Now, I'm not one to dredge up things from the past, but I'd at least like to have a hint of what I'm dealing with. It seems to affect everyone so strongly…even you."

Aggie turned to her. "I have nothing to say about the Winters family."

"That's just it. I don't remember Tommy ever talking to

me about anyone named Winters. And I guess that bothers me because I thought I knew all of Tommy's friends."

Aggie dropped her shoulders and stared at a space on the wall for a long moment. The lines in her face deepened into a regretful look and she placed her outreached hand on Becky's cheek. "You *did* know all of Tommy's friends. All of his *real* friends."

Aggie's hand was cool against Becky's cheek. But her touch sent an emotional wave through Becky. It was easily the most affection Tommy's mother had ever shown to her. Becky closed her eyes, struggling to keep her composure, struggling not to think about how long it had been since someone who mattered had touched her tenderly.

But she wouldn't let that distract her from the topic at hand.

"So, they *were* friends at one point?" Becky asked.

Aggie nodded. Her hand fell away. "Yes. But…it was so long ago. Really, Rebecca, you don't need to worry about this. It's over and not important anymore. Just remember Tommy the way you do. Leave other people's opinions out of it."

"Opinions? The Winters family has a bad opinion of Tommy? Why, if they were friends? I don't understand."

Aggie turned away, her face like a stone. "It was a horrible time, Rebecca. They made accusations. Spread rumors. Ruined Tommy's reputation. They were angry, jealous people. Not surprising when you consider their father embezzled money from the Kirkpatrick foundation."

What? Becky's head was spinning. "Their father embezzled money from the Kirkpatrick foundation? What happened to him? Is he in jail?"

"No, he died in a plane crash when all this happened. My husband dropped the charges against him."

"And what about Tommy? How could they ruin his

reputation when their own father stole money? It doesn't make sense. What did they accuse him of?"

"Really, Rebecca, just put this to rest. Trust me." She sniffed and turned her head even farther away so that Becky couldn't see her tears.

"Mrs. Kirkpatrick, you are ready for lunch, no?" Dyanna the housekeeper bustled into the room.

"No, Dyanna. I seem to have lost my appetite. I'm going to lie down in my room for a while. I have a sudden headache." Aggie glanced back at Becky, then moved to the back stairs leading to her rooms.

Becky unclenched her fist and forced herself to breathe again. Tommy had told her that he'd had a reputation with the girls before he became a Christian. She, of course, had not asked for details. He'd told her enough for her to know that he'd been reckless, drank too much and made many stupid decisions. But she couldn't imagine what horrible thing the Winters family could accuse him of. Tommy could never have been mean or violent or malicious. Never.

This all had to be some sort of horrible misunderstanding. A terrible, stupid misunderstanding.

But how?

That Becky didn't know. But she wasn't going to put this to rest. Not when it concerned her treasured Tommy. And Justin, too. He seemed so sad and tied to this thing in the past. Becky couldn't imagine what it was that had them all so tight-lipped—Aggie and Katie, too. But she wanted to know. She wanted to know this secret between the two families—the secret that seemed to be a hold on her friendship with Justin.

Chapter Nine

"I still don't want to work with her." Katie put the Sunday dinner dishes away with more force than necessary.

"It won't be that bad." Justin shrugged. "And I'll be there some of the time working on the set."

"Yeah, a lot of help you are," Katie said, mocking his voice. "Welcome to our church."

"Now, now, Katie. At least she was there at church, and so was Aggie," said their mother, Jenna Winters. "That says something about Becky Kirkpatrick. Aggie hasn't been to church since Tommy left town."

Katie looked ready to argue the point, but the ringing phone interrupted her. Katie took the cordless phone out on the porch after answering, leaving Justin and Jenna alone.

His mother motioned to the seat beside her at the kitchen table. "Sit down here and talk to me. I've hardly seen you since you've been home. Tell me about things."

Justin went to the kitchen table and sat next to his mother. "Not much to tell."

"That's not what I heard from Mrs. Richardson."

"You mean Matt's mother? Matt, the medic?"

She nodded.

Justin shot his mom a playful look. "And here I thought the army gossip was bad."

"Come on. Tell me what's going on in your life." His mother eyed him the way she used to when he was in grade school.

"Hey, you're the one who talked to Matt's mother. Why don't you just tell me what it is you want to talk about?"

"I heard you had trouble out on your emergency call."

Justin stared into his mother's round brown eyes. What was he supposed to tell her? That her son could barely do his job these days?

"I also heard that the patient was none other than the woman of the hour, Tommy Kirkpatrick's widow."

Justin pressed his hands on the top of the table and started to push himself up. "Well, sounds like you know the whole story, so I think I'll go outside."

"Not so fast, Dr. Winters. Have you had any other episodes?"

"Yeah, Mom. I have." Shame anchored him to the chair. He rubbed his forehead and looked away. It was one thing to fail in front of friends. Or mess up for yourself. It was a whole other feeling to let down your mother.

"What happened?" she asked.

"It wasn't a panic attack. I didn't lose time or anything. But at the clinic last week, an older man came in. He was a hemophiliac. He'd cut himself on a wire fence in his garden. I treated him and he was fine. I was fine. Then he left and the nurse came in to throw away the bandages and clean up the table…and I don't know. I looked around and saw all that blood and I sort of lost it."

"You cried?"

"Like a baby." Justin shrugged. "I can't remember that I've done that since Dad died."

"Exactly. Sometimes we need to cry. It's part of healing.

Have you had a chance to do that since the rebel incident? Have you cried over Gentry?"

"No. I try not to think about it."

"How about over Tommy?" she asked.

What? He hadn't expected that question. His eyes shot up and met hers, looking back at him steady and even and full of tenderness. She touched his hand. "You loved Tommy. So did I. So did Katie. It's okay to mourn, to say goodbye."

Justin's mouth was so dry it wouldn't open. He didn't know his mother had come to terms so well with the past. She looked so peaceful there talking to him. Unlike himself. Inside him, there were so many emotions swirling he could scarcely breathe.

"You know, if you're going to get over all this angst," she said, "you're going to have to talk through what happened with someone. Don't you think?"

"Like with my mom?"

"No. With someone who understands what you're going through."

"There's an army therapist. I talked to him before I was released."

"And?"

"Okay, Mom. I'll think about talking to someone."

"Good. So now…" She patted him on the shoulder, stood and walked to the kitchen counter to pour herself another cup of tea. "Tell me what you think of the young Mrs. Kirkpatrick?"

Justin whipped his head around to where his mother stood. Her conversation couldn't have surprised him more. She looked back at him waiting for an answer.

"Well, I don't— I don't think anything about her," he said. "I hardly know her. I took her to the hospital and then saw her at the school the other day. She seems nice, I guess. Not that I care, though. I mean, she's pregnant and was married to Tommy. It's not like I'm going to be friends with her or anything."

"Yeah, you seem really uninterested." His mother gave him one of those irksome nods that said she didn't believe him. "She's quite beautiful. I'd never seen her before today at church."

Justin gulped. Was he supposed to respond to that? "Yeah, she's okay."

"Okay? She's okay? Do you need your eyes checked, Justin Paul Winters, because if you think she's just okay, then you can't see straight. She's stunning."

"Sure. Fine. She's gorgeous. What's your point?"

"No point. I just want you to be careful."

"Careful? What are you talking about?"

"You know what I'm talking about."

Justin sat back in his chair and folded his arms over his chest. This was getting silly. "Really? I know what you're talking about…"

"I saw you talking to her after church. I saw the way you looked at her."

"I also talked to Mr. Elfkin and Pastor Dean after church."

"Yes, but you weren't fidgeting and blushing when you talked to them."

"Come on, Mom. It was hot in there."

"Uh-huh. They didn't kiss you, either."

Justin leaned forward and clapped his hands together. "And that's what this is all about? Don't be ridiculous. She felt her baby kick for the first time and she got all excited. It was nothing."

"Might have been nothing to her." His mother leaned forward and lifted an eyebrow. "Be careful, Justin. You've been through a lot. You're still *going* through a lot. Don't go looking for something more than you can handle. I don't want to see a child of mind heartbroken over a Kirkpatrick. Not again."

Katie stood in the doorway to the porch, nodding her head in agreement to his mother's words. She'd obviously been listening to the entire conversation. "I'm over Tommy. Now I just want to put the whole Kirkpatrick clan out of my life and out of my head. But you, Justin... You seem..."

"I seem what?" Justin filled with anger now. How dare they accuse him of whatever it was they'd thought he'd done wrong. He was the one who took care of them. Protected them. Fought for their happiness and safety. He pushed away from the table and stood. "I was nice to her. Told her I was sorry about Tommy's death. So what? You two are making a big deal about nothing."

"Are we?" his mother asked.

Justin grabbed his jacket from a hook on the wall, made sure the keys to his Jeep were in the pocket and moved toward the door. "This is ridiculous. I liked it better when we were talking about my panic disorder. I'm going out for some air."

Justin drove aimlessly. Trying to clear his head. Trying to make sense of the confusion inside him. The pain of losing Gentry, the ache of Tommy's betrayal, the fear of his inability to practice medicine without panicking—there was so much jumbled inside him. He passed buildings and homes and parks and forests and countryside. Some places were new, like the coffee shop. But most were old like the high school, the hospital, the lake. Places that had been there for as long as he could remember. And remember was exactly what Justin did. Taking in the sights and sounds and smells of Glendale, bits and pieces of his youth played out through his cluttered mind.

He drove and drove. And although his time on the road

had subdued the intensity of his emotions, as for understanding any of them, he had made no progress. Memories of Tommy brought mixed feelings, as did thoughts of Becky. Flashes of war and hurt people filled him with angst and guilt. Maybe his mother was right. He probably needed to talk to someone. He certainly needed to settle in his mind once and for all how much of Gentry's death had been his fault. He checked the clock on the car. It had gotten late.

But at the next crossroad, Justin didn't turn toward home. Instead, he chose another road through the countryside. And not just any road; it was the one that would lead right in front of the Kirkpatricks' large, gray-stone house. Right in front of the majestic Greyfield. It was part of clearing his thoughts, he rationalized. After the conversation with his mother, it was natural that he explore his connection, past and present, to the Kirkpatricks. Right?

Right. How much of *that* night had been his fault? Did he even want to know? No. It didn't matter. He left them alone and that night changed all of their lives.

Justin slowed his car as he passed under the old chestnut tree marking the edge of the Kirkpatricks' property. Images from the past circled through his mind—games of tag, chestnut wars, tree forts, swimming, baseball games. He and Tommy, despite the tragic end to their friendship, had shared some great times.

The Jeep barely rolled forward now as he passed the old pond. There he and Tommy had fished, skipped stones, skinny dipped, raced to the gelatinous bottom and back. That had been gross. But good training for the army. Justin laughed aloud. Beyond the pond, there was a field of cattle belonging to a local farmer. Amazing they'd only been caught cow tipping once.

A loud horn blew. Justin glanced into his rearview mirror. Moving at his snail's pace, he'd started blocking traffic. He pulled over to the shoulder, letting the cars behind him pass. Idling the engine, he sat there taking one last glance around the land, then he hit the accelerator to merge back onto the single-lane road. The Jeep lurched forward then sputtered and the engine died.

Justin turned the key again. Nothing.

Great. Stupid Jeep. Always breaking down. It was one thing to drive it to the hospital and back. Places he could get home from easily. But not here. A drive through the country-side—and not just any countryside: Greyfield—meant he'd have a hard time getting home unless he could get the Jeep to start.

Justin tried the engine again. A loud screech squealed out from under the hood. Then nothing.

Perfect. He dropped his head to the wheel in despair. He couldn't think of a worse place to get stuck. But that's exactly what he was—stuck and stranded in front of the Kirkpatricks'.

Justin pulled his cell phone from his pocket and started to dial his sister. But how would he explain his location? He couldn't.

He put his phone back and popped the hood. Maybe if he rattled a few wires, the car would start again. He walked around to look at the engine. He stared at it. Located the bat-tery. Wiggled a wire or two. Went back to the driver's seat and tried the ignition again.

Nothing.

"Having some car trouble?"

Justin swallowed hard at the sound of Becky's voice. He hadn't expected someone to spot him there so quickly. In fact, he was a good half a mile from the actual house. What was he going to tell her? How could he explain the fact that he was broken down in front of her property?

He slid back out of the car and smiled sheepishly. "Hi, Becky."

"Hello, Justin." She stood on the sidewalk, wearing the same dress as she had at church. On her feet, however, she'd exchanged the espadrilles she'd worn earlier for a pair of tennis shoes. "I was out taking a walk and I heard this horrible screeching sound. I thought an animal was in trouble."

"No. Just me. And my broken-down Jeep." He kicked at the front tire.

She lifted a brow. "That probably fixed it."

"Actually, that was just to make me feel better." He smiled.

"Did it work?"

"No... I guess you're wondering what I'm doing in front of your house?"

She pressed her lips together and shrugged.

"I was out for a drive. Trying to clear *my* head. Guess it ended up being a bit of a drive down memory lane."

Her face relaxed a bit as if to accept his explanation. "I've had a few of those myself recently."

"Anyway, I pulled over looking at that old chestnut tree and when I tried to get back on the road, the engine just died on me."

"Oh, the chestnut tree! I love that old tree," she said. "Tommy told me there used to be a swing there, a—"

"A tire swing." He nodded, picturing it in his own mind. A smile broke out over his face. "Tommy and I would challenge each other to see who could jump out of it, the farthest away from the tree, or see who could touch the highest limbs. We pitched a tent there one night and... Man, a lot of good memories."

She looked away, uncomfortable. "You want me to call someone for you? Give you a ride to a shop?"

His mother was right—he needed to leave this poor

woman alone, which would be easy to do since she didn't want to talk to him. "Right…the car. Well, thanks, but there's not much open in Glendale on a Sunday." He pulled his cell phone back out of his pocket. "I'll phone a friend. And don't worry. Sometimes it just needs a little rest and then it starts right back up."

"That sounds practical."

"What can I say? I like to live on the edge."

"Really?" She lifted an eyebrow. "I had you pegged more for the quiet and cautious type."

She had him pegged? She had thought about him? His heart skipped a beat. "Yes, well, don't tell the guys in my unit. They'll think I've gone soft."

"Our secret." She smiled. "Speaking of secrets, I'll bet you and Tommy had plenty."

Secrets you don't want to know. He held his breath, praying that was not where this conversation was going.

"You two must have had a lot of fun here."

"So, you believe me now? That we were friends?" he asked, still holding his breath.

"I talked to Aggie." Becky sucked on her cheek and looked away. Uncomfortable seconds passed. How were they going to get through the next several weeks with all this tension?

"She told you the whole story?"

She shook her head. "No. She got a headache. But I'm patient. I'll learn the rest of it."

"You know, Becky, the past is past. We could just leave it there."

She smiled reluctantly. "I'd like to think that but it doesn't really work that way, does it? I mean it's something that happened a long time ago but it still seems to be upsetting a lot of people. Otherwise, we would talk about it."

"Or, we don't talk about it because you've been through

a lot, because Tommy is gone and the memories will just upset you."

"Can we talk about why you're home from the army?"

Justin was starting to think he'd left his mother's house and conversation just to end up here and start it all over again. "I don't really want to talk about that, either."

"Right." She put her hands on her hips and started to walk away. Justin didn't know what Aggie had told her but it was enough to make her skeptical toward him, and he didn't like the way that made him feel. Didn't like it at all.

"Right. I'll just get back to work on my car, then."

"Okay." She nodded, already walking back toward the house. "Good luck."

Justin watched as she moved away. His heart raced. Why did he want to go after her? He knew why. Because he liked her. Because she was hurting and he cared. Because he wanted to be friends with her. Get to know her better. And yet he shouldn't. He had too much baggage. Too much pain from the war, and from Tommy....

He looked down at his phone. He should call Matt or his sister. Not ask Becky for help. But then he'd have to explain why he was broken down in front of the Kirkpatricks' home and he didn't want to do that, either. Convenience, he told himself as he started after her, knowing that was not at all the reason he tracked after her for help.

Chapter Ten

"So, you're really just going to leave me here?" He trotted up behind her.

"Thought you were going to phone a friend." She looked back over her shoulder. She was smiling, relaxed.

"I was. But I'm thinking through some other options now." He caught up to her. His head said bad idea. *Get yourself home without her help.* Some other part of him followed her like a lost puppy.

"Ah." She placed a finger on her cheek. "Such as?"

"Taking you up on your offer to help. I don't know anything about cars."

"Really?" She laughed. "I thought in the army you could assemble bombs out of detergent and make keys from paper clips and stuff like that?"

"Yeah, well, I'm the flight surgeon. I know the insides of people. Not the insides of cars."

She stared at him with a doubting expression.

"Okay. Never mind. I'll go back and wiggle some of the wires."

"You really don't know how to fix it, do you?"

"Uh…no. And sometimes once she cuts off, she doesn't start again for days."

"Hmm. I don't think Aggie will put up with you being on her lawn for days. Perhaps I should send Mr. Jimenez out to you."

"And who is Mr. Jimenez?"

"The gardener. But he knows about engines, too. I'm sure he'd look at it if we asked him to." She stopped. "But for my help, I get to ask you for a favor."

"A favor? Do I get to know what the favor is?" Justin stopped, scratched his head, his heart pounding a little faster. Was she going to ask him for the truth about Tommy? He hoped not.

She pretended to think about it. "No."

"So, I'm agreeing blindly?"

"Yes." She smiled.

"You're enjoying this." He pointed at her.

"I am." She nodded. "So, what will it be? Favor for favor? Or I walk back to the house and you wiggle wires?"

"Favor."

"Then let's get your car fixed."

Justin followed Becky to the garden shed, wondering two things. One, what he'd just promised to do for her. And two, how much trouble it would cause him and his heart that he was falling head over heels for one Mrs. Tommy Kirkpatrick.

"I can't believe Mr. Jimenez." Justin patted the dash of his Jeep. "He whipped this engine apart and threw it back together so fast. And listen to it. Sounds perfect."

"I think he enjoyed doing it." Becky glanced down at the school registry sitting in her lap.

"So, where to for this favor of yours?"

"William Gaines's home. Twenty-four hundred Vine Street."

"Okay. I know where that is." Justin steered his Jeep proudly off the grounds of Greyfield.

"Mr. Jimenez seemed pleased to have some company and conversation." Becky smiled. "I can imagine that Aggie is pretty boring to work for. She has one routine. It never varies. In fact, I'm sure today threw the poor housekeeper off terribly since we went to church."

"So, how is it? Living with Aggie?" Justin turned onto the main road leading into town and toward the school.

Becky didn't answer him right away. No one had asked her about that. No one. Not even her friends from Atlanta had asked about how life with Aggie had been. She looked over at him, wondering exactly how much to share. Aggie acted as if he were the enemy. But he didn't seem like the enemy. He seemed like a friend, even when he talked about Tommy. Maybe especially when he talked about Tommy.

She pushed some of her waves back from her face. "Aggie's been good to me. We had a rough beginning. I wasn't the kind of girl she wanted Tommy to marry, but she's been kind to open her home to me. I don't mean that she's easy to live with, but coming here was the right thing to do. I am more certain of that today than ever before. I was so pleased she went to church today."

He nodded. "So, why'd you move here? You must have a ton of friends and family back in Atlanta."

"I left some friends in Atlanta." She shook her head. "But I don't have any family."

Justin's face paled. "I'm sorry. That was presumptuous of me."

"It's okay. I'm young not to have parents. My dad left home, didn't look back. My mom passed away when I was in college. And Tommy…" She stopped, wiped a tear from her cheek. She didn't want to go on with the conversation, especially if Justin really thought something ill about Tommy.

Something she knew couldn't be true. Something inside her said that Justin needed to know the truth. That Tommy was not whoever Justin believed. That Tommy was a good and kind man. Some part of Justin must know that. He'd looked so happy, talking about that old tree. What could have happened to tear that friendship apart? "Tommy wanted me to stay with his mother until the baby was born. So that I wouldn't be alone. And he really wanted us to go to church together."

"He must have loved you very much," Justin said without looking her way.

"And I loved him."

Justin leaned back in his seat, letting out a long sigh. "Must have been so hard to say goodbye. For him. I—I can't imagine."

"It was hard, but Tommy was at peace." She took a deep breath, glad that the conversation had continued.

Justin frowned at her words, shaking his head back and forth. "At peace? How was he at peace? He was so young. He would never get to see or hold his own child. Where's the peace in that?"

Becky turned and tilted her head. His comments surprised her. "Don't you see death in your line of work? Haven't you seen someone who was okay with dying? And you must risk your life sometimes being in the Middle East. Are you not at peace?"

"It's different. We know the risks. We expect gunfire and bombs. But here at home, it…" Justin sighed. "I don't know. It seems like our lives should be safe."

"But being safe and being at peace aren't the same thing, are they?"

Justin shrugged. "I guess I've had trouble with all that lately."

"Well, Tommy knew that his life was in God's hands,"

she continued. "So, he was at peace in his heart. And he was okay with the path that it ended on."

Justin stared back at her with a blank expression. "And you're okay with all this? You're not angry? You don't feel cheated? Lost? Angry?"

"You said angry twice."

"I know. I just can't imagine what you've been through."

She smiled and nodded gently. "It's been hard. And I've been all those things—angry, sad, lost... Both times. With my mother and now again with Tommy. But I'm working on acceptance. But it's difficult. Part of me lives in fear of losing anyone I care about." *Like this precious baby growing inside me.*

Justin turned onto Vine Street.

She pointed to the brick rancher home at the end of the block. "Look. There it is. Twenty-four hundred. Right there on the corner."

Justin pulled his Jeep in front and parked against the curb. The grass was overgrown. The paint peeled from the shutters. And weeds grew up from the cracks in the front walk.

Becky double-checked the address. "At least, that's what my register says."

He gave her a reassuring smile. "You said they just moved in. Maybe they haven't had time to work on the house."

She nodded, taking in the shambled appearance of the home. It was not at all what she'd expected of William's family. The boy was so well-read, clean-cut, nicely dressed and well mannered.

Justin sat for a long moment staring at the dash, a deep frown and faraway look on his face.

"You ready?" She touched a hand to his knee.

Justin reacted as if she'd shocked him with a couple of

bolts of electricity, sitting up straight and at attention. His face filled once again with color. "Sorry. Just thinking about the peace thing."

He reached his hand to the keys then pulled them away as if they were hot to the touch. "You know, I'm almost afraid to turn her off."

"We can always call Mr. Jimenez. He won't mind." A grin spread over Becky's lips, despite her wariness toward Justin. And he didn't seem angry toward Tommy. Perhaps Aggie had been mistaken about the Winters family.

He pulled the keys from the ignition. "You think we should have called first?"

"Probably." She hopped out of the car, pretending to be confident about the unannounced visit to William's home, when actually it was the first time she'd ever shown up at a student's house without a scheduled meeting. Then again, this was different. This student had had an accident and an asthma attack on her watch. Finding out how the mother felt about that seemed an appropriate measure.

Justin stepped out of the car, fiddling with his keys before he closed the door and walked around to her. His eyes grazed over the neglected home and garden then came to rest on her. "So, why did you want me along for this? What exactly is my role? Teacher's aide? Handyman working on the set?"

"You're the doctor. I don't know anything about asthma and sprained ankles." Becky studied him. She liked his quiet strength and his tamed energy. He was so different than Tommy. Tommy would have barged inside and worried about introductions later. Justin wanted to think it through. It was interesting that they'd been friends. Justin was much more cautious, observing, quiet. Strong. In fact, he seemed all goodness and kindness. She felt comfortable with him. Maybe she shouldn't. "Actually, I hate parent confrontations. Especially ones with angry parents."

"And she did look angry on Friday." He smiled.

Becky nodded. "So, it will be good for a doctor to emphasize the importance of notifying teachers about William's condition."

"So, I'm here for my medical savvy?" he teased.

"Yes. I also want to find out why he's quitting the play. Now, quit worrying and come on." Becky stepped up to the door and knocked. He followed.

Mrs. Gaines answered. A look of dismay washed over the woman's face but was quickly replaced by a smile and a wide-opened door.

"Sorry to intrude, Mrs. Gaines. We probably should have called first," Becky started.

"No—no, it's okay," the woman said, motioning with her small hand for them to come inside. "I'm glad you're here."

Justin and Becky followed her into a small sitting room, sparsely furnished with a modest sofa and two armchairs. The walls, painted a buttery shade of yellow, held a haphazard display of drawings. On the floor were unpacked moving boxes. But despite the disorganization, the home was clean and had a warm feel to it.

"Who's the artist?" Justin asked.

"These are all William's. He's a gifted child. Takes after his father," she said proudly.

"He is very talented," said Becky, looking at the pieces. She didn't know much about art but these pen drawings, mostly of airplanes, looked good enough to have been done by someone much older than William. "I really like this one. The shading is so detailed."

Justin nodded. "Yeah. Look at this cockpit. I've actually flown one of these before. He's captured every knob, every level... It's perfect."

"That's one of my husband's planes." Mrs. Gaines gestured to the covered armchairs.

They all took a seat. There was no sign of William, which was exactly what Becky had hoped for. A moment alone with the mother to see what was really going on with William's sudden loss of interest in the play.

"So, Dr. Winters and I came over to tell you how sorry we were about the incident on Friday. We feel terrible that William got hurt at practice."

"Well, thankfully, you both acted quickly the other day or things could have been worse. It's been difficult—the asthma, the new school, a new town…" Mrs. Gaines forced her lips into a smile. "And William wants to do everything himself. He doesn't realize the dangers. I'm not sure anyone does."

Justin cleared his throat. "How long has William struggled with the asthma?"

"The attacks started years ago…but it's been worse since we moved here." She waved a hand through the air.

"Lots of changes when you move. It might be hard to narrow down the triggers," Justin said. "But you're controlling the situation with medication, right?"

"My husband started a new business here. Our insurance doesn't cover all of his meds. We can't afford the medicine William needs to take. Only the inhalers to stop the attacks."

Justin and Becky exchanged glances. No wonder Mrs. Gaines was so concerned. And embarrassed. Perhaps pride had kept her from informing the school. She wondered what Justin was thinking from a doctor's perspective.

"It's just temporary, of course," she added. "Once things get going, we'll be able to purchase the medication again."

"Have you tried any alternative medications that might be less expensive?"

"He tried one prescribed by his former doctor. It made William jittery. But his asthma is fine as long as he sticks to classes and drawing and nothing too stressful." She looked defensive now and searched the air as if to find another topic.

So was he fine or was he worse? Seemed to Becky that maybe Mrs. Gaines did know what the problem was and she wasn't divulging it to them.

"Is that why he isn't going to participate in the play?" Becky asked. "You know he tried out for the lead. He was very good."

Mrs. Gaines tucked a lock of hair behind her ear and glanced toward the back of the house. "He does like the theater. Where we lived in the city, he was a regular in the community productions. He's had a lot of experience. Loves it. But…with his asthma, he should take some time off. His father thinks so, anyway."

"Did his asthma bother him in the other plays he participated in?" Justin asked. He, too, must have picked up on her conflicting reports of William.

Mrs. Gaines looked uneasy.

"In any case," Becky added quickly, "with Dr. Winters at most of the practices you could relax a little knowing a doctor is on hand."

"I don't know. His father needs his help after school."

A screen door at the back of the house slammed hard and the sharp sound cracked through the home like a whip. A nervous look fell over Mrs. Gaines. She stood abruptly and folded her hands together. "Thanks for coming by, though. Very kind of you."

Justin and Becky stood, following Mrs. Gaines's lead. "Our pleasure. Thanks for seeing us."

"You know, Mrs. Gaines, I work at the hospital clinic and we sometimes provide medication for patients with certain…

well, with certain needs. I could help you with the paper-work. If you want to come in, I'll be there tomorrow. We could request William's medical history from his former doctor and see what to do for him."

"I don't know." She walked quickly toward the front of the house. "I'd have to speak with William's father."

"Of course." Justin smiled.

A man's deep voice broke through the room. "Well, we lost the Brandt account and the Harveys'. If I lose one more, then…"

The tall, thin man stopped as he appeared at the door. He smelled of sweat and engine grease and frowned deeply at the sight of Justin and her. "I didn't know we had company."

"This is William's new teacher," Mrs. Gaines said, shifting her weight nervously.

"Hello," Mr. Gaines said with a tight mouth.

Becky suddenly realized what a silly idea it had been to visit William's home unannounced and before talking to other teachers about his home life. She had no idea what she'd walked into—and she'd brought Justin along, to boot. She turned to him, desperately searching for the words to explain their uninvited presence. But Justin looked as thrown as she felt.

Time to make a quick exit and apologize for the intrusion. What had she been thinking? Or had she been? Perhaps being with Justin muddled her brain?

Chapter Eleven

Justin watched Becky pale and tense as Mr. Gaines stepped into the room, until William came swinging in behind him.

"Dr. Winters!" The kid's face lit up. "And Mrs. K! This is my new teacher, Dad! Mrs. K. She's the one working on the play."

"Well, we've already talked about that, son," his father said. "Don't start up again."

"Come on, Dad. The play is going to be great. I really want to do it." He looked desperately at Becky. "That's why you are here, right? To talk my dad into allowing me in the play."

"No. Dr. Winters and I just came to check on you," Becky responded. "See how you were getting around on those crutches. But there is another tryout tomorrow. We would love to see you there if you change your mind."

"Mrs. Kirkpatrick said that William was really good at the lines," Mrs. Gaines said to her husband.

Mr. Gaines grunted. "That's great. If I didn't need help at work, it would be fine. But right now I do and you can't do it with your rheumatism, Martha. So quit making me out like I'm the bad guy here. It's just one stupid play."

The blood drained from Mrs. Gaines's face, clearly embarrassed that she'd been caught in her attempt to make them believe their decision about the play had something to do with William's asthma.

William seemed to ignore the whole scene, as if he'd heard it a million times before. "Hey! You guys could stay for dinner. Mom made spaghetti."

"Oh, no," Becky said, feeling an uncomfortable warmth flush her neck and face. "We both have to get home, William."

"Nice to meet you both," Mr. Gaines said. "Sorry about the play. It's just the way it is."

Justin turned back to William's mother and spoke in a low voice, "Remember, I'll be at the clinic tomorrow."

She did not respond, but closed the door quickly behind them. Justin and Becky walked in a hurry to the Jeep, both of them taking a deep breath as they neared the passenger door.

"The poor kid has to work? He's eleven. I guess being in the school play is trivial compared to all that's going on in there."

"I know." Justin nodded. "Sounds like money problems."

"Yes, it does. I can relate to that. My mother and I had our fair share of those," Becky said.

"And you? Are you okay? You look pale." He leaned in and touched her shoulder.

"The smell made me a little nauseous. But I'm fine now."

Justin opened the passenger door to his Jeep and offered his hand to help Becky in. She hesitated, slowly accepting his hand, which made the contact with her all the sweeter. Their eyes connected. The intensity of her gaze on him made his legs feel weak. He needed to get a grip. She was right—the past was between them. He looked down at her pregnant belly. And that was her future. They had a lot standing between them. It was silly for him to entertain any sort of feelings for her, probably even friendship once she found out the truth about everything. But someone needed to explain all that reasoning to his heart, because the logic wasn't getting down there. He liked Becky Kirkpatrick. He liked her a lot.

Justin squeezed her hand tight, as he helped her inside then hurried around to his own door. Once inside the car, he stared at the dash for a moment. He'd forgotten about the Jeep. He slid the key slowly into the ignition. "Now, to see if she starts?"

The Jeep started up on the first turn. Justin threw his head back and laughed. "I've had everyone in town look at this Jeep. I don't know what Mr. Jimenez did differently, but whatever it was, it worked. I feel like I could drive her across the country now."

"Or back to the army?"

"Yes." Justin stiffened. Did that bother her? That he would be leaving? He sensed it in her tone. And it gave him hope to think he wasn't alone in his feelings for her. That maybe she cared for him, too. But he would be leaving. There was no doubt about that. So why wasn't he feeling quite as ready for that as he should? He knew why. Justin pressed his lips together at the thought of his own budding emotions. He pulled the Jeep away from the curb and headed back to Greyfield.

Becky stared after the Gaines's home as they drove away. "I wish I could help William. I feel like I need to, but I don't know what to do."

"I think the first thing to do is to make sure William gets the medicine he needs."

"Well, I can't do anything about that."

"No, but I can." He smiled. He liked being able to do something that would make Becky happy.

"Right. You can. You're a doctor. See? It's great that you came along today." She returned his smile. "And then what?"

"Then, maybe I can talk to his dad. If he's into planes, I might be able to connect with him."

"Would you do that?" She smiled. "Could you?"

"I want to do it. Plus I want to see his Cessna. I haven't flown one of those in years."

"Do you fly often?"

"No. I log hours and I'm licensed, but it's not a huge part of my work." *In fact, right now I'm scared to death of flying in a small craft, which is a bit of a problem for a flight surgeon.*

"Very cool. I guess you're the first pilot I've ever actually met. So, you could fly Mr. Gaines's plane?"

"Sure." *If I could get over my fear.*

"So how did you get into aviation medicine?"

"My dad flew a plane for Mr. Kirkpatrick. There's a little runway here in Glendale. It's probably where Mr. Gaines flies in and out."

"Aggie told me your father died in a crash. I didn't know he was the pilot. I'm sorry."

He shrugged. "He had an aneurysm while flying."

"And so that's how you got into the medicine part?"

"Yes. That and I like to help people."

"I've noticed that." She smiled, and Justin ached to reach his hand over and caress her soft, sweet cheek.

Instead, he stared intently at the lines dividing the highway. "So, speaking of doctors and medicine, how have you been?"

"Hanging in there. Still have a few months to go."

"True, but you must be getting ready, right? Thinking of

names, and that sort of thing. Have you fixed up a room for the baby at Greyfield?"

"No, not yet. No name ideas, and no nursery decorating. I don't even know that I'll stay with Aggie after the baby is born."

"Oh. Will you go back to Atlanta?"

"I don't know. Maybe. I'm really waiting on God to know what to do next."

"And are you scared to be a parent?" *Like I'm scared to do my job.* This conversation was more about him than about her. He wondered if she'd figured that out already.

"Do I seem scared?" She chuckled a bit.

"You don't seem scared of anything."

She burst into laughter. "Well, maybe I should be on the stage, because the truth is I'm petrified. Are you kidding? All that responsibility. A whole helpless life in your hands, depending completely on you. You must feel like that all the time though, huh?"

"Like what?"

"As a doctor, you must feel like others depend on you. The pilots and the men in the division or the people in the clinic."

Justin cringed. Could they really depend on him? No. That's why he was home. It was like he had nothing to give these days. Nothing but his own fears in the way of everything. "I don't know."

Becky blinked at his terse response. "You don't like being home, do you?"

Justin blew out a long sigh as he pulled to a stop in front of the Kirkpatricks' home. "My unit is still deployed, working without me. Doesn't feel right."

Becky clutched her bag in her fingers and put a hand on the door, ready to exit the car and go inside. "I don't understand. Why did you take leave if you want to be deployed?"

"I didn't *take* leave, Becky. I was *put* on leave. Mandatory leave."

"I didn't know." She stepped out of the car quickly. "I'm sorry. It's none of my business."

He gave her a nod, teeth clenched. She started to close the door.

"Wait. Becky."

She turned. The soft folds of her long dress flowed around her legs in the evening breeze. The small roundness of her belly protruded just slightly at her middle. "You forgot your jacket. It's here in the backseat." He handed it to her but purposely didn't let go as she reached for it.

Should he tell her why he was on leave? Tell her what had happened in the Afghan scrub? He hadn't shared the details of what had happened that night with anyone. Not really. He'd not told anyone how it had affected him, so why would he tell her? And yet as he looked at her he was compelled to do exactly that.

"I'm home because I'm drained. But I want to go back… it's just that…well, I've got to get my head straight first."

"Tommy's death drained me, too." She looked him hard in the eyes, pulling her jacket from his hands. "Especially when I look at the whole big picture of starting over. It's overwhelming."

"So how do you cope?"

"I don't look at the big picture right now. I deal with smaller moments. You should try it."

"How?"

"It's easy. Just focus on shorter tasks. Just like we did today. Fixed the Jeep. Talked to William's parents. I figure if I can get through some of the smaller moments, then one day I'll be able to tackle the whole picture again."

He nodded, but he wasn't so sure he understood. "Good night, Becky."

"Good night, Justin." She closed the door to the car and walked up to the house.

Justin watched her disappear into the house, thinking over her words. Maybe that was the problem—he was thinking too hard about the big picture. Then again, maybe he was just a big-picture kind of guy and his problem was that the picture he was seeing right at that moment had a lot of Becky Kirkpatrick in it.

But it shouldn't. He and Becky could have no future. His family would never approve. Aggie would never approve. And deep down, Justin wasn't sure he approved, either. Could he really care for the woman who had pledged her life to Tommy? Could he care for their child?

Justin didn't think so.

Becky wrapped the jacket Justin had handed her around her shoulders and made her way through the house toward her bedroom. *What a strange day.* She sat at the edge of her bed, removed her shoes and looked down at her swollen feet. Not a pretty sight. Pregnancy sure did crazy things to the body. She spun around, elevating her legs.

Then she checked her blood sugar. Perfect. And no insulin. Dr. Klein had thought she might need it, but so far the diet was working and making her feel stronger every day. Even emotionally she felt stronger. Going to church had been wonderful.

Feeling the baby move had been wonderful—the baby she hardly dared to dream or think about. Becky found herself still too afraid of the potential to lose her, and concentrated more on her own health and body. But the movement inside her today... This baby was real, whether she dared dream of her or not.

Yet even Justin had asked her about the baby. Justin... It almost seemed as if they were becoming good friends. Obviously Justin wasn't the perfect friend. There was still this weird past hanging over them. This past that no one wanted to tell her about. The past that her own husband had kept from her. She still believed that Tommy had had a reason for not sharing it all with her. Maybe one day she would understand. Maybe not. She was at peace with it.

Mostly.

Lord, maybe I don't have to know exactly what happened. But it's clear this thing from Tommy's past affects Justin and Aggie and Katie. Lord, I pray for these old hurts to heal. Bring peace to all our hearts. And Lord, I pray for William and his family. Please touch them and provide whatever things they need. And thank You for this baby growing inside me, for the joy of feeling her move and knowing that You are taking care of her. Taking care of us both. Help me to overcome my fears and believe it, Lord. Amen.

She let out a long sigh, stretched and started for the bathroom. A warm shower, a cup of tea and a good book would be the perfect way to end the evening. Slowing as she passed the set of shelves that flanked the hallway to the bath, she searched over the titles of books belonging to Tommy—comic books, graphic novels, spy novels, textbooks. She ran her fingers over the dusty bindings. A collection of Shakespeare's comedies. A large, unused dictionary. A calculus book. A yearbook.

Her finger paused.

A yearbook? Hmm. She didn't remember ever looking at one of Tommy's yearbooks. She'd looked through all those photo albums a few nights ago. But she hadn't thought of a high school yearbook. And here was a whole set of them— *Glendale High School Dreams.*

She pulled all four books from the shelf and carried them

to the bed, spreading them across her fluffy, paisley duvet. This could make for some very interesting reading tonight, she thought. Especially as there was only one high school in Glendale. Perhaps, Tommy and Justin would have been there at the same time and, finally, she would see some pictures of them together.

Becky picked up the edition of Tommy's senior year and began thumbing through the pages. Almost immediately, she found a picture of Tommy and Justin together. They were side by side all padded up for a football game ripping through the cheerleaders' formation and stretched pep sign. Tommy was smiling and waving to the crowd. Justin looked serious, his pensive eyes focused ahead, full of determination and grit.

A few pages later, she came upon more photos of them at their homecoming. The captions read: *Justin Winters awarded most valuable player. Tommy Kirkpatrick, Homecoming King.*

Justin was dancing with a tiny girl who could hardly get her arms around his neck. Becky looked closer. The girl was the plump and bubbly nurse, Melodie, from the hospital. Although slightly thinner in high school, there was no mistaking her face.

The picture of Tommy made her laugh. He had a crown on his head and was making a silly face for the camera.

On the next page, Tommy danced arm in arm with a girl who looked silly in love with him. And there was something familiar about this girl, too. Becky studied the picture, but couldn't quite place her. She had long dark hair and a knockout figure. Becky read the caption below. Then read it again. *Homecoming King Kirkpatrick dances with Freshman Princess, Katie Winters.*

Oh, boy. Maybe she was in a bad episode of *Dallas* after all? So, Katie and Tommy had been a fling or they had dated. And so what? No way that that could be the whole problem. Everyone would have been over a high school romance by now. That had been twelve years ago. There had to be more for everyone to make such a big deal of it.

Becky opened the next yearbook and then the next. They were all filled with pictures of Tommy and Justin. Justin was usually playing a sport and looking serious. Tommy was always with a different girl, smiling and laughing. They did make an odd pair of friends. And other than that, Becky couldn't draw any more conclusions. At least, she could finally see with her own eyes the proof of Tommy and Justin's friendship. Now, the question remained why Tommy had kept it a secret. There had to be a reason.

Looking through the last yearbook, a yawn escaped her lips. Yep. Long day. Time for that shower and some sleep. She gathered the books together again and took them back to the shelves. One of them slipped from her fingers. As it hit the ground, a small green envelope popped out from between the pages.

Strange how she'd flipped through the entire book and not noticed it. But there it was, just as old as the pages it had been hidden in. She lifted the green square from the floor. It was sealed and stamped, but not postmarked. It had never been mailed. She quickly recognized Tommy's handwriting on the front.

It was addressed to Katie Winters.

Becky stared at the envelope. She studied it, turned it over in her hands, put it down on the shelf. Only to pick it up and start the process all over again. Should she open it? Would it contain answers to her questions about Tommy's connection to the Winters family? That past no one wanted to tell her about. Including Tommy.

Becky put the letter back down. She showered and got ready for bed then she picked up the letter again. How she wanted to open it and read aloud Tommy's words. How *had* he felt about Katie? She wanted to know.

Perhaps Aggie and even Justin were trying to protect her from this truth they thought she couldn't bear. And she *had* just prayed for peace over her ignorance. But the truth was she wanted answers.

She deserved answers.

She flipped the envelope back over and ran her nail under the seal. She ripped into it about an inch then stopped.

What was she doing?

This wasn't her letter. It was Katie's. And Tommy had decided not to send it. Who was she to open it?

Nobody. And so she wouldn't. She couldn't. It would be disrespecting Tommy's and Katie's privacy. She did wonder why Tommy hadn't thrown it away if he didn't intend to deliver it. Should she give it to Katie?

So many questions swirled in her head.

Becky was tired. She returned the letter to the annual and placed it back on the shelf. Maybe everyone was right. Maybe it was time to move on and simply leave the past in the past.

Chapter Twelve

Katie stood at the edge of the stage with her clipboard and script. "Since I was sick on Friday, we're going to have everyone read again for parts this afternoon. And we'll post the cast tomorrow."

There was a short moment of silence, then boos and hisses sprang from the children in mass force. Becky had figured as much. On average, kids were not a patient lot. She watched as Katie whistled and pleaded, but she could not get the students quiet.

Becky stood to the side of the stage and searched through the large room, looking at each face then sighed when she realized that William had not shown up to the tryouts. Justin wasn't there, either. She'd been afraid of that, too. While their afternoon together fixing his car and visiting William's home had been enjoyable, there remained that secret past between them, this unease caused by their divided loyalties. Justin might like her company as she enjoyed his, but he was guarded and oftentimes awkward. Under these circumstances a friendship could only be so deep. Not to mention he'd told her that his leave was only temporary, that he was eager to get back to his unit. Becky wouldn't let herself get attached to another person who was just going to leave. She'd been left behind too many times already.

Anyway, she was completely overanalyzing the entire thing. Which was nothing. For all she knew, he'd dropped her off and had a date with the best-looking woman in Glendale. She only hoped he was able to get William his medicine and talk to Mr. Gaines. That was all. Becky shook her head and decided to put her silly thoughts away and focus on practice.

But that was difficult. One look at Justin's sister and she thought of the high school yearbook and the little green envelope with Tommy's letter to Katie—the one she couldn't decide what to do with. Read it. Give it to Katie. Leave it be. She didn't know, but for now, the letter would stay right where it had been, tucked away inside Tommy's yearbook.

Katie continued to struggle with the children. Slowly, Becky walked up on the stage and stood beside Katie. Justin's sister looked indifferent to her approach. But the students soon changed their boos and hisses to a succession of pleas— *Mrs. K, tell her we already tried out and we were good.*

Becky smiled as they quieted down a bit. "I don't know what all the fuss is about," she said. "You were wonderful on Friday. You'll be just as wonderful today. Let's start with Callie as Roxane and Blake as Cyrano and Jason as Christian. Top of page ten."

Katie's eyes widened. Becky couldn't tell if she was angry or in shock that the students quieted down and did exactly what she'd asked. But the tryouts proceeded. Katie occasionally spoke to her, but seemed to avoid her as much as possible. More than ever Becky wanted to know the truth about Tommy and these people who used to be his friends.

The hour was long, much longer than on Friday. Her only encouragement was that many of the students she'd had in mind for certain roles had already shown improvement. On the other hand, none of the boys could pull off the Cyrano lines with the same amount of flair as William.

Trying to concentrate on the last two students reading lines on the stage, Becky sensed someone behind her.

"Mrs. K? Is it too late?"

"William, you're here! No, get up there and read." She handed him a script. She was so glad to see him. She'd prayed so hard that he would get to be a part of this.

The other students on stage worked William into the scene. And he was brilliant. Even Katie dropped her attitude and looked over at Becky with an approving nod.

When they finished, Katie took the stage and explained when she would post the cast and when the regular rehearsals would begin.

Again, Becky sensed someone behind her.

Justin?

A second later, she caught him approaching in her peripheral. The fact that she'd known it was him before she saw him sent a warm tingle across the back of her neck.

"I came to see if William was here," he whispered as he slid into the seat beside her.

The warmth in Becky's neck trickled through her whole body now. But she didn't look at him. Instead, she kept her eyes ahead on Katie, dismissing the students. Katie seemed to keep one eye on them, as well.

"Yes." She shrugged. "He came. Late. But he came. And he was great. Even Katie noticed. Did you talk to his dad?"

"No and his mother didn't come to the clinic, either. So I brought a medicine he could try. I thought he might be here."

Becky searched the room for William. "He was just on the stage reading. But I don't see him now."

"Yes, I don't see him, either," Justin said.

Becky frowned. "Are you thinking what I'm thinking?"

Justin nodded. "You said he was late. I'll bet he went home after school then snuck back here for the end of the tryouts."

"Oh. I hope not. I want him in the play but only with parental permission."

"How about another quick visit to the Gaines's home? I should give the medicine to an adult, anyway. Want to go with me? You could check with his mother about the play."

Becky nodded, although she worried about what Katie would think of them leaving together. Still, she followed him to his Jeep. William didn't live far from the school, yet in the short time it took to get there Becky grew anxious and her head filled with questions about the past and the letter and Tommy's secret. It was all she could do to keep the discovery to herself.

Justin parked against the curb and the two of them walked up the front steps and knocked at the door.

Mrs. Gaines opened the door but only enough to show her face. "Yes?"

"I didn't see you at the clinic."

"I didn't want William to miss school."

"I brought a medication for William to try." Justin handed over a small white bag. "These are just samples. But if this helps William, then schedule a visit and the clinic will help you get this medicine at a reduced price. If it doesn't help, there are a few others he could sample."

With hesitation, she reached for the bag in Justin's outstretched hand then stopped. "Pete wouldn't want me to take this without paying for it somehow."

"Your son's health is more important than maintaining

standards." Justin pushed the bag at her. "William needs this medicine, Mrs. Gaines. It's free. Take it."

"Thank you." She took the bag and started to close the door.

"Wait, Mrs. Gaines, what about the play?" Becky held her hand to the door to keep her from closing it.

"What about the play? His father doesn't want him in the play. End of story."

"And yet he was at the tryouts today," Becky said. And already at home. She'd noticed his crutches leaning against the wall in the foyer.

William's mother stared back at her. She did not look surprised in the least at Becky's report. She had to have driven him. It was the only way he could have gotten back and forth to the school so quickly.

"Your son has great talent," she added.

"I know he does," she said. "But his father, he wants him at the hangar. Some days I won't be able to get him to the practice."

The three of them stood silent for a long minute. They all wanted the same thing but didn't know how to get it. Becky couldn't think of a solution. It would be too hard to run practices with a lead that wasn't there most of the time.

"Well…what if he could do both?" Justin broke the silence. There was a twinkle in his eye and a spirit of hope in his tone. Becky liked this side of Justin—the one with his guard down.

"I don't see how that's possi—"

"I'll work something out with your husband, Mrs. Gaines. At least, I'll try. Just get William to practice. Okay?" Justin said.

"I don't know. I don't think you can get him to change his mind."

"Can I try?"

She shrugged. "Of course. If you can find a way to make my husband feel like he's done the right thing by moving here, then by all means. For now, I need to race William over to the hangar. We're late." And she closed the door.

"What was that all about?" Becky asked as they walked back to the Jeep.

"I have an idea." Justin helped her in then walked around to the driver's side and climbed in. He smiled boyishly at her. "I think I can do a favor for Mr. Gaines. And maybe he can do one for me, as well."

Justin was on a mission and Becky liked his spunk.

"Any chance you're going to share?"

"Not until after I get you some food. Have you tested lately?"

"Yes, just before practice." She checked her watch. "But you're right. It's time for me to eat."

"Good, because I just got off a long clinic shift and I'm starving."

She stared at him for a long moment. "Are you saying we should go out? Like go eat dinner together?"

He laughed. "Yes. Like go eat dinner together. Why not? We're friends, aren't we?"

"Sometimes it seems like we're friends. Sometimes there's this big bad past between us."

"Yes, but that's the big picture. You and I are going for those smaller moments. Like dinner." He grinned and wiggled his eyebrows at her.

He was teasing her, but she was relieved to hear that her pathetic advice hadn't put him off. And she liked the idea of having a friend. Still, it didn't seem like the best of ideas, their going to a restaurant together. What would Aggie say? "I don't know, Justin. I need to get home and grade papers and stuff."

"Hmm. Well, here's the thing. I've heard this rumor that you have never been to Tennessee Bob's Famous Ribs."

"Tennessee Bob's? Sounds like a diabetic nightmare."

"Oh, no. It's pure culinary genius."

Becky laughed and relaxed back into her seat. Maybe dinner would be fun. And when was the last time she'd had fun? "You're right. I haven't eaten there. Then again, can't say I've been much of anywhere since I've been in Glendale."

"I knew it. Well, you can't live in Glendale and not have eaten at Tennessee Bob's. So we have to fix that."

"Oh, really?"

"Yeah, I'm pretty sure there's a fine or some sort of penalty for it."

"Uh—huh."

"Come on, Becky. I don't want to have to call the authorities on you."

"You wouldn't."

"I would."

Chapter Thirteen

Tennessee Bob's was packed and loud and not the least bit romantic. Justin had planned it that way so that they'd both feel more at ease in each other's company. But the fact he'd been planning to do anything with Becky Kirkpatrick was enough to fill him with anxiety. Not to mention question his own sanity.

But Justin was drawn to her. And keeping his feelings reined in, as he knew he should, was proving to be more difficult than he anticipated. Already, he was lost in her smile and easy conversation.

"I've been a middle-school teacher ever since I graduated from college. A lot of people burn out with this age group, but I love it," she said with a glow in her crystal blues. "How about you? How did you decide army?"

"I saw an army air show when I was a kid. Loved it. Had every kind of model military plane available. Knew I'd join the army as soon as I turned eighteen."

"Seems like you would have become a pilot?" she asked.

"Yeah, I love to fly, but you need to be a bit of a cowboy to fly for the military. Medicine is a much better fit for me."

"I can see that."

"Tommy was more the pilot type," he said.

She looked up fast at the mention of her husband, as if eager to hear more.

"Except he didn't like to travel much," he added with a smile.

"You knew him very well." She laughed and put down the last empty rib bone. "These were really the best ribs I've ever had."

"Told ya."

She cleaned her sticky hands with the wet towel and looked across the table at him with a frown. "Can I ask you something personal?"

"About Tommy?"

"Would you actually tell me about Tommy?" She looked him hard in the eyes.

"Tommy was great." He smiled softly. "Fun-loving, athletic, a good student and usually a good guy, but sometimes—"

"But sometimes he did stupid things?"

Justin nodded, wishing he could let go of his hurt from Tommy. But he could see that if this conversation continued, he'd end up hurting Becky. And he did not want to do that at all.

"He told me."

Justin hung his head low. Tommy obviously had *not* told her. She didn't know about Katie. And he didn't want to tell her. In fact, he hated even thinking on the past. He wished it all away so that he could develop a friendship with Becky untainted by others' bad decisions and a hurt still buried deep inside him. Not to mention his own guilt for his role in the tragic event.

She smiled. "I know Tommy was with a lot of girls before he committed his life to Christ. We've all made mistakes, Justin."

Well, one of them was Katie. The words were right there but Justin couldn't say them. One word on that subject and their friendship might be over. "When was it that Tommy changed?"

"A year or so before I met him. After he moved to Atlanta. I don't know what he did that upset you and your sister so badly. But I'm having a hard time thinking that the Tommy you knew and the one that I knew were so different. Maybe he didn't know God so well as he did later. He admitted he didn't make it a priority. Anyway, I hope you and your sister can accept that Tommy loved God, he cared about people, and maybe forgive him for whatever it was he did to hurt you."

"I'm glad we met, Becky. It's making me work on that." He nodded, again marveling at her strength and wisdom.

"I'm glad we met, too. But that's not what I was going to ask you."

"Oh." Justin leaned on his elbows over his empty plate and propped his head up on his fists, smiling. She didn't want to talk about Tommy and the past. That was more encouraging to him than she could have possibly imagined. "Okay. What then?"

"Well." She laced her fingers together and set them on the table. "What I was wondering is… Is it because you're away all the time, you've not married? Or did someone break your heart?"

Heat rose to Justin's cheeks. He reached for his soda and took a long drink.

Becky waved her hands in the air nervously. "Sorry. I've embarrassed you. That was too personal. Forget it."

"No. No. It's fine." He tried to reassure her but she still looked uncomfortable. And boy, if she wasn't cute when she got flustered. "It's just that no one has asked me that in a long, long while. Uh…" He had to think back. "So, I was engaged once. It didn't work out. Since then, I've tried dating a few women from home, but the long distance is tough."

"Does that bother you? Not having a family?"

Justin looked around the noisy restaurant at the many families dining there, considering her question carefully. "No. I do want a family, but being a flight surgeon is what I'm meant to do. I'll have to meet someone who can understand that and cope. I haven't so far."

"And your engagement?" she asked.

Justin looked across the table at Becky, her blue eyes sparkling with interest. He took a deep breath. He could fall so deeply for her. If only things were different... If only Katie hadn't... "Well, when we were in medical school, it seemed perfect. But then we graduated. Set a date. I signed another contract with the army and she moved to L.A. to do cosmetic surgery."

"And that was it?" She laughed.

He laughed, too. "Oh, no. There was more. I wanted a family. She wanted a goldfish. I wanted to do clinic work. She wanted her name in America's Top Doctors. I liked the Braves. She liked the Yankees. That sort of thing."

"Wow. So, you didn't exactly have the same vision."

"Not even close. We started to argue about everything. When she told me she didn't want to get married in a church, I cut my losses and ran to Afghanistan, which is right where I'm supposed to be."

Becky's smile faded, replaced by a more reflective look. "So, why are you home, if you feel you are supposed to be there?"

"That's—that's a good question." Justin swallowed hard, his eyes darting away from hers then back. "But wait a minute, what about you? Were you ever in love before you met Tommy?"

Becky shook her head. "No. I never had time to date. I was always working and trying to get through school."

He stared at her soft face for another long moment, feeling too much. So much for his idea of having a friendly dinner. What he felt was much more than friendly. His mother was right. He cared. And he liked caring. There was something so peaceful and steady about her. She had a calmness that flowed out of her and into those around her. He'd seen it first with the students and now he felt it at work on him. But he couldn't be more than friends with Becky. Not now. Not ever.

He was glad when the waiter moved in and placed the little leather folder with the bill into his hands.

"We should split that." She pulled a credit card from her purse and offered it.

Justin looked over the folder at her. "Afraid not. That's another Tennessee Bob thing. The first time you eat here, someone else has to pay for your meal." He glanced up at the waiter, who nodded in agreement.

"I'm pretty sure you're making that up, but I'll be nice and play along." She put her card back, wiped her mouth with the white cloth napkin and set it aside. "Thank you for dinner. This was a real treat."

"My pleasure." As she looked into his eyes again with a certain measure of gratitude, the emotions pulled again at Justin's heart. He caught himself glancing down to her lips. Yikes. That was definitely beyond friendly. Dinner alone with Becky had been a bad idea.

Justin signed the check, popped up from the table and walked briskly out to the car. Becky could hardly keep up pace with his stride.

"You know you said you would tell me what deal you're going to work with Mr. Gaines after dinner and it's after dinner, so…"

"Did I say that?" he teased, amazed at how quickly she could pull him back.

"Yes, you did. So, come on. Spill it."

"Uh… My idea is to get Mr. Gaines some business. I have a feeling he wouldn't need William around to do the odd jobs if he could afford to pay the staff available at the hangar."

"What if that's not the issue?"

"I don't know. What else could it be? The kid is eleven. He couldn't be that much help."

"True."

"So, first I'll go down to the hangar. Check out the situation and feel it out. Then I'll make a few phone calls and hopefully get him some business. I'll let you know how it goes."

"That doesn't sound like much of a plan."

"But if it works, then you'll see William at rehearsal. Isn't that enough?"

"That would be great." She smiled and Justin again loved the idea of doing something that would make Becky happy.

"You should do that more often," he said to her.

"What's that?" she asked.

"Smile."

Chapter Fourteen

Justin couldn't believe it. He was flying Mr. Gaines's Cessna. And it was the best feeling in the world. Soaring over green hills, blue lakes, great forests and rivers and streams. Somehow during his time in the Middle East, he'd lost sight of the fact that the whole world wasn't a desert filled with hate and war and suffering. He'd forgotten how to enjoy this beautiful earth that the Lord had given him. He'd been so caught up in duty and helping others, he'd gotten to a place where he was so drained and full of fear that he had no time to reflect and recharge.

If it weren't for Becky, he wouldn't have ever figured that out. Her advice to take the small moments. It was so perfect.

"Woohoo!" He glanced over at Pete Gaines and his son, William, who sat in the small passenger space behind the cockpit.

"You sure you're not a full-fledged pilot? You fly this thing like a cowboy." Mr. Gaines chuckled.

"No, sir. I'm just a doctor with a few hours under my belt. But thanks for letting me log in some flight time. I'd really gotten behind." And that was the truth.

"You seemed a little nervous at first, but I tell you what, you are some kind of pilot," Pete said.

"As good as Dad," William said.

"Well, it feels great to do this again. Thanks."

"I like your proposition," he said. "I'm not so keen on my son being in a play but as long as he can keep up with his work and you're going to drive him over to the hangar... Well, the truth is I can't say no to all those clients you're promising to get me."

"Yes, sir. There's a lot of retired military in Glendale and they all want to fly from time to time and keep up their hours. You charge a reasonable fee here in Glendale and they will be very happy not to have to drive all the way to Nashville to do the same thing."

"Like I said," Mr. Gaines repeated. "I like the proposition. Things have been tight. Too tight."

"And you'll come see the play, right, Dad?"

Mr. Gaines smiled but did not answer.

Back at the hangar, Justin paid him for the gas, the air time and for landing and takeoff privileges with a large wad of cash.

"That's double what you owe me, Doctor. I can't take that from you." Mr. Gaines tried to hand back half of the cash.

"No, sir. I called three other companies that offer flight time and that's actually one hundred dollars less than what they would have charged me to do the same thing. Keep the money, Mr. Gaines. You earned it."

Mr. Gaines held the roll of money up to his face. "You mean, these friends of yours will also pay this for flight time?"

"Yes, sir. Like I said, I know three men planning to call you this week. And through word of mouth you may get more. They will want to fly at least twice a month."

The man's eyes teared slightly. "You know what this

means? I'll be able to make the payment on my crop-dusting plane. How can I thank you?"

"You could come to William's performance."

He nodded. "I'd do that, anyway. How about something for you? A free flight? Maybe with that beautiful teacher friend of yours?"

Justin could feel himself blushing. "Now, you might be on to a pretty good idea there, Mr. Gaines."

Becky couldn't believe how fast the weeks went by now that she was teaching again and working on the play. Instead of crying herself to sleep at night, she found herself dozing off in the evenings with a red ink pen in her hand and a lapful of essays to read. Instead of conforming to whatever schedule Aggie had predetermined for the day, Aggie was now checking with her and adjusting accordingly. And healthwise, she had to admit she'd never felt better. Life once again had rhythm and purpose and joy.

Except when she saw Justin.

When she saw Justin, she felt a little off course—a little unsure of herself, a little breathless, a little preoccupied, a little energized…and a lot happy. She looked forward to those moments at church and, like now, at play practice. And she hated when they ended. Even if they'd done nothing more than say hello to each other, when they parted she felt lonelier than ever. She supposed she *was* lonelier than ever.

She was already sad that the play would be over in a month or so and she wouldn't see Justin so often. Of course, he'd be leaving to go back to his unit anyway. She wondered when that would be. And how alone she would feel without knowing if she would see him again. She had this wonderful baby to think about, but that frightened her, too. Even though she wouldn't admit it, she was hopelessly in love with her unborn child, and so afraid she would somehow be taken away, like everything else in her life...like Justin.

Putting away her scripts, she looked over at him painting a door to the stage set with one of her students. He was showing the kid to go with the grain of the wood and not from side to side with the brush. The child accidentally sprayed him with a wayward stroke. Paint flicked upward into his face. Justin laughed, shook his head and showed the kid again how to stroke the paintbrush. As if sensing her eyes on him, he turned toward her and smiled. She looked away but it was too late, he'd seen her and was now approaching. That mixture of energy and uncertainty flipped through her body in a mad rush.

"I've been meaning to ask you to dinner again," he said. "But they upped my hours at the clinic and I've only had three nights off. How about Friday?"

She looked up at him, her heart pounding. "I don't know. By the time we're finished with rehearsal, I'm ready to prop up my feet and call it a day."

Katie walked by the two of them. An unhappy expression covered her face at the sight of the two of them talking.

"And then there's that problem," Becky added.

"I can handle my little sister. And I'd really like to spend some more time with you before I go back to my unit, Becky. Not to mention I have something pretty cool planned." His face was lit up like a child's on Christmas morning.

He'd already planned something? Yikes. Didn't that make it a date?

William came to stand beside them, a huge grin on his face. He looked up at Justin. "Did you ask her?"

"Just now, champ."

William glanced at her with a knowing expression. "I know what it is!" he teased. "I know where you're going."

"Oh," Becky said, amused by Justin's openness and his

developing friendship with William. "Is it some place that I would like?"

"For sure," William said. "I wish I could go."

Becky looked up at Justin to see how he would respond.

"That's a great idea, buddy," Justin said without hesitation. "You're welcome to come if your parents don't mind."

William jumped. "On a Friday after school, I'm sure they won't mind. Come on, Mrs. K, you have to come, too. Otherwise, I'll bet Dr. Winters won't even go."

"That's right," Justin agreed.

"I'm thinking about it," Becky said, trying to sound very noncommitted.

"Remember, dinner is just a small moment," he teased.

She lifted an eyebrow. "Using my own words against me?"

"Whatever it takes." He flashed that smile that melted her into tiny droplets.

"Okay." She returned his smile now. "Dinner with you and William, Friday after rehearsal."

Justin strutted off with William at his heels. Becky swallowed hard. While a little part of her wanted to spend time with him, there were so many reasons she shouldn't. His sister's clear anxiety whenever she saw Becky and Justin together. The secret past. Aggie's dislike of the Winters family. Not to mention that even though they were merely friends, she felt disloyal to Tommy and the memory of him. But it was for that very reason that she would go. On Friday, she would ask Justin to tell her the whole story about what happened between Tommy and him. She wanted him to leave out nothing. And perhaps then she'd know what to do with the letter to Katie and perhaps she'd know what to do about her friendship with Justin.

Friday's rehearsal came quickly. Becky hardly had time to think over her dinner with Justin. And suddenly, as she saw him across the stage at work on the set, she felt a bit anxious and guilty about the arrangement. Even though William was coming along, dinner with a handsome single doctor to whom she was no doubt attracted did not seem like a small moment. It seemed like a big date—and she wasn't ready for that.

Becky swallowed hard and helped Katie distribute a handout to the students about costumes, makeup and the final rehearsals. Justin cleaned up the work area and laughed with a bunch of the kids around him. It seemed like no time before the students had been dismissed and he was heading her way. He looked pretty fine in his dress slacks and button-down shirt. She glanced down at her pair of skinny jeans and loose baby-doll-style blouse. Casual Friday. Maybe that had been a bad idea. But he hadn't told her what they were doing and since he said William was coming she… Well, she hadn't thought to dress better. Now, she worried and was mad with herself for worrying.

"William needs to get something from home." Justin smiled. The gleam in his eye said he was up to something. "Can we swing back and pick you up?"

Relax. Breathe. Becky could feel the blood racing through her. "Do I have a choice?"

"Nope. You will break William's heart if you change your mind now. See you in a minute."

Justin and William headed out and Becky continued to help Katie straighten up the auditorium. Katie had yet to relax around her and Becky really hated the thought of spending the last few weeks on this play still not speaking to one another.

"I thought the practice went well," she said.

Katie shrugged. "They need to work on projecting more."

"A few of them." Becky folded the last of the chairs on the

stage and turned off the house lights. "The sets look nice. I don't remember having anything so elaborate when I was a kid."

"We have some generous patrons." Katie picked up the stack of scripts, took a few steps toward the doors and stopped. "And Justin is good. Though I think we both know he's not putting in all this work for *my* sake."

"Excuse me?" Becky looked over at Katie who avoided eye contact with her, as usual.

"You heard me. Look, I don't know what you want from my brother, but if you are looking for some kind of link to Tommy, you won't find it in Justin. Our family hasn't had anything to do with the Kirkpatricks for twelve years. I think it should stay that way."

"I have no idea what you're talking about. Your brother and I are friends. It's got nothing to do with you or your family. Or Tommy."

Becky grabbed her bag and headed for the door. She hoped she could beat the tears.

Chapter Fifteen

Becky raced out of the school building as Justin pulled into the teacher parking lot. Something was wrong. Becky looked upset and was headed straight for her car. He drove up next to her.

"Are you okay?"

She stopped. Her head and shoulders dropped low. She didn't answer him.

"Okay, I can see that you are not okay. Becky, is this a pregnancy thing or something else?"

"Something else," she mumbled, fumbling through her large bag.

"So you feel okay? It's not your blood sugar?" he asked.

Becky had been fine when he'd left rehearsal, which meant something had happened after he'd gone and left her alone. No, not alone. With Katie… Justin frowned at the thought of his moody sister. "What happened?"

Becky lifted her head now and turned to him. She'd regained her composure. He imagined she was an expert at that trick. "I don't think I'm up for an outing this afternoon."

No. No way. He was finally ready to talk to someone about what had happened and his sister was not going to steal that from him because she wanted to pretend the Kirk-patricks didn't exist. "Does it have something to do with the fact that I left you alone with Katie?"

Her eyes went wide. The electric blueness of them pierced his senses.

"You're pretty good," she said. "First try."

"I'm sorry, Becky."

"It's okay. I just tried to talk to her, be friendly. But it didn't go so well."

Justin climbed out of his Jeep. "You want to talk about it?"

"No. But I want to know the whole story." She looked up at him. "It's time."

"I agree. Come with me today, Becky." He started to walk her to the passenger door. "There are two things I want to tell you."

"What about your sister? What about our plans with William?"

"Katie will understand. And so will you. We'll keep our plans with William. Come on. I've been planning this all week. Actually, William will be crushed if you cancel."

"William will be crushed?" She smiled now and even let out a chuckle.

"Please?"

She hung her bag back over her shoulder and climbed into his car.

"I hope we don't regret this." Her voice was a whisper.

Justin reached out, taking one of the long strands of her golden hair in his hands. It felt like silk between his fingers. And the sweetness that struck through him as he touched it shocked even him. He'd wanted to do that since the first day he saw her. "No regrets, Becky. Just honesty and friendship."

"I'd like that."

Justin liked the sincerity in her eyes and her voice. Now, he would be brave and tell her his story. He steered the Jeep toward the hangar.

"Speaking of William, where is he?" she asked.

"He's getting things ready."

"And what would he be getting ready?"

"You'll see." He smiled. "It's part of my story."

"Your story?"

"Yes, well, it has to do with why I'm home…." He glanced over to see if she looked even remotely interested.

She was smiling. "You have my full attention, Doctor Winters. You know how long I've wanted to know your story."

Justin relaxed his hands on the steering wheel. It was going to be easy to talk to Becky, so easy. But would it be easy for her to hear? "It's not a pretty story. Are you sure you want to hear it?"

She smiled sweetly in that way of hers, so open and accepting. "I wouldn't have asked if I didn't want to hear it."

Justin nodded. "Yeah. So, a few months ago, a young pilot named Gentry was flying me into a 'HOT' zone to treat some Afghan rebels that had been wounded by an insurgent attack. We thought the area was clear but…"

"It wasn't."

"No. There were snipers at the landing. A one in a million shot. One of them hit Gentry as he started to touch down. He took the plane right back up into the air. But he was hit in the stomach and started bleeding out quickly. I needed to land the plane somewhere and work on him. But he wouldn't let me. He said it was a trap and we'd both die."

"Wasn't there a copilot?"

"No. It was a small two-man plane. Anyway, he was determined to get far away from there, so I tried to close up the wound while he flew us back but he was bleeding so badly.

Finally, he told me to take over. Get us back. But he wasn't going to make it."

"So you tried to save him?"

"Yes. I went back to the landing strip, and mind you, I have some flying hours but landing in the dark without lights on a tiny strip…"

"Wow."

"And Gentry was right. The landing was mined. Blew off the tail of the plane and set the whole thing on fire."

"But you got out?" Becky seemed almost breathless waiting for the next piece of his tale.

"I did. I got both of us out and I took off with him in my arms. I ran and I ran. I kept looking for that rebel base, hoping to find it before those snipers found us. But Gentry…"

"He died?"

"I couldn't save him. All my supplies blew up in the plane. I had nothing. I tried to put pressure on the wound and bind it with my shirt. But he died in my arms. And I felt like a failure and a phony. It was like everything I stood for was meaningless and made no difference."

"But you didn't do anything wrong. You can't blame yourself for a sniper hitting the pilot."

He shook his head. "I had pushed for the mission. It was my fault."

"You wanted to help people. There's nothing wrong with that."

"Gentry is gone because I wanted to help people. He had a wife and two children. He was going to start teaching after this deployment, spend more time at home."

"I'm sorry." She covered his hand with hers. "He was your friend?"

Justin nodded. "But I think he died in peace—like Tommy. And he sure tried to save my hide. Even at the very end he said to tell his boys that the Lord knows they are strong enough to take care of their mother."

"That takes a great faith. Sounds like he was a great man."

"He was."

"And you forgive yourself for pushing for the mission?"

"I don't know if I forgive myself, but you're right I was trying to help and that is what I do."

She squeezed his hand. "So how did you get back?"

"Well, that's the crazy part. I don't even know. I don't remember much of the next few days." He turned to her to gauge her thoughts. "I was in a trance. I somehow got to the rebel camp. Apparently, I treated some of their people and in return they drove me back to my division."

"Wow."

"Wow is probably not the best word for it." He smiled. "That's when I completely shut down. I couldn't work. I was scared to even look at a plane. I had to take a round of sedatives to get home. I had panic attacks and nightmares, all day and all night. Sometimes the rebel base days come back to me in little flashes. I don't know if I'll ever piece it all back together or not."

"I'm sorry. But you must be better? You've been working here. Since you've been home. Right?"

"I've been handing out bandages, Becky. But, yes, thanks to you, things have improved."

She made a doubtful face. "Thanks to me?"

"Yes. The day you went to the hospital was a breakthrough. I worked in that E.R. for six hours so that you could be admitted. I had panicked at your house and I felt I had to make amends. So, you gave me a goal. Without it, I wouldn't have made that step. So, yes, thanks to you."

"I'm glad you're getting better. And you do make a difference."

"Yes, I really am better. Slowly, through working at the clinic, I've been able to control the panic and examine the fears more rationally. And I'm very glad. I want to get back to my men."

"And how about the flying?"

"Well, that is better, too. Also, thanks to you, for putting me in touch with the Gaines family. So good, in fact, that I was going to show you."

And as if he'd perfectly timed the story, they pulled into the Glendale airstrip and headed toward Mr. Gaines's small hangar. The Cessna was already out and ready to go. William stood beside the left wing, waving and holding the picnic basket Justin had packed for their excursion.

Becky's eyes went wide. "You're going to fly?"

"*We* are going to fly," he corrected. "The three of us. That is, if you want to. I cleared it with your doctor. He said you would be fine. What do you think?"

Becky remained silent as he parked the Jeep to the side of the hangar. He walked around and helped her out. William came running over.

"Mrs. K, she's all ready to go. Dr. Winters is going to take us to the mountains for a picnic dinner. How cool is that?"

Becky smiled, but Justin saw the hesitation in her eyes. William apparently did, as well.

"Don't worry, Mrs. K, Dr. Winters is a great pilot."

Some relief softened Becky's expression. "So, you've already flown since…?"

Justin laughed. "Yes. Three times this week."

"Well, okay, then." She nodded and the three of them headed to the plane, but Justin felt light enough to fly without it. Telling Becky about his experience had lifted his spirits—or was it just spending time with her that did that to him? Maybe both.

He just hoped they'd still be friends after she heard the rest of the story. The part about Tommy.

Chapter Sixteen

William had been correct in saying that Justin was a good pilot, but Becky was still a little nervous flying in the small craft. It helped her put into perspective the horrible night Justin had just recounted. She tried to imagine how terrifying and helpless he must have felt. What a brave and amazing man he was—one she'd like to know more. If only he wasn't leaving soon....

The Tennessee Smoky Mountains rolled under them, green and bursting with new spring life. Justin landed in a private airfield near Pidgeon Forge. A big white Hummer came to meet them at the end of the strip. They deplaned and walked to the Hummer. A gray-headed man with broad shoulders and a cockeyed grin waited for them.

"Major Winters," he said to Justin.

"Captain," Justin said, reaching a hand out. The older man pulled him into an embrace. He turned to Becky. "This is Captain Miles Peirce. Retired F-14 pilot from the 101st Army Airborne. This is Becky Kirkpatrick."

Becky shook his hand and smiled.

"I have heard a lot about you, my dear." There was a twinkle in his eyes. "You must be pretty special to keep

Major Winters away from the job. He's been known to be the army's most un-eligible bachelor."

Un-eligible? Becky frowned. Had Justin forgot to tell her about a girlfriend? The mere suggestion of it set her on edge.

"He means I'm married to the job," Justin explained.

Becky couldn't stop the blush, nor the strange relief she felt at knowing Justin wasn't attached to another woman. Like it mattered. She was getting ready to have a baby. He was getting ready to leave. She and Justin were just friends. And maybe not even that.

"No need to get embarrassed, Miss Becky. I'm just giving the major a hard time. He's a stand-up guy. Just never gives the ladies much of a chance."

"It's hard to compete when you're surrounded by fighter pilots everywhere. I get lost in the crowd."

Becky doubted that somehow.

Justin looked to William. "And this is William Gaines. His father is the one I was telling you about with the new business and this is their Cessna."

"How do you do, William?" The captain tousled the boy's hair. Then he looked to the plane behind them. "I will check her out, but she looks about perfect for lessons and logging in some hours. Here are the keys to the Hummer." He handed a key ring to Justin and pointed to the other side of the airstrip. "Just follow that dirt path at the end of the field and that will take you to the river. Enjoy."

Sitting in a wooden gazebo overlooking the Little Pidgeon River, Becky, Justin and William enjoyed the sandwiches, chips and juice that Justin had packed for their outing. Lovely dogwoods and fern grew along the steep river banks. The water ran swift and clear over large stones and the sound of rushing water filled the air. A family of beavers popping in and out of their home provided some live entertainment. William especially enjoyed watching. And after he'd finished eating, he hopped on his good foot down to the bank, rolled up his jeans and stuck his feet in.

"It's cold!"

"Good for your ankle," Justin yelled back. "Keep it in for a while."

Becky eyed Justin. "Trying to keep him away?"

Justin nodded. "Always looking for a moment for you, Becky."

"I can't imagine anyone wanting a moment with me." Becky looked down at her belly.

"You are a very attractive woman. The fact that you're having a baby and still look like a supermodel is all the more appealing."

He couldn't be serious. Could he? "I'll try and take your word on that. But it's hard."

"Do. It's the truth. And I'm not much on handing out compliments."

"Now that I believe." Becky took in a deep breath of the fresh mountain air. "It's beautiful here. Tommy and I talked about getting a cabin in this area."

"Yes, there are some really beautiful places up here. I was pretty excited when I called the captain the other day about William's dad and he asked me to bring down the plane. I thought you might like it here. Plus, it made me remember the last time I was in the Smokys."

"Oh, yeah? Sounds like another story."

"It is quite a story. I was with Tommy." He laughed. "We drove down here looking for a party that some girl had invited him to. We never found the party. So instead we went fly fishing and camped in the back of my truck. It was one of my favorite times with him."

"Tell me what happened, Justin. What did he do that was so unforgivable?"

Justin looked her in the eyes, his face in a frown. "We were hanging out one night. I let Katie come with us for some reason. That was my mistake. She'd always had a horrible crush on him. But she had started dating this guy Brad so I figured she was finally over it. Anyway, my dad called. Mr. Kirkpatrick had these investigators at our house going through all of our things. Dad called me to come get my mother out and take her to a friend's house because she was so upset and nervous. And he didn't want me to tell Katie what was going on."

"This was about the embezzlement?" she asked.

His eyes widened. "So you do know some of this?"

"No. Not much. Go on."

"I left Katie with Tommy, took my mom to a friend's house on the other side of the county with her crying all the way there. Then I drove back to Greyfield and I found Katie and Tommy…"

"In bed?" Becky wasn't surprised. She had already guessed where the story was going, especially after seeing the pictures of Tommy and Katie at the dance together.

He nodded. "Katie was only fifteen."

Becky nodded. "I guess I understand why you would no longer be friends, but it was twelve years ago. Can you understand that Tommy changed when he became a Christian? And he was sorry for those things that he did."

"Yeah, well, I do get that now. Thanks to you, Becky. Now that I know his life took a different path, I want to make peace in my heart over Tommy. I really loved him. But Katie… No, Katie has never gotten over it."

"It was twelve years ago. She should move on."

Justin looked away.

"There's more, isn't there?" Becky was almost afraid to ask.

He nodded. "Katie got pregnant. She ran off, lied about her age and had an abortion."

The sandwich Becky had just eaten unsettled her stomach. It was all she could do to keep it down. At the same time, she filled with anger and disbelief. "And Tommy was blamed for that? Are you sure it was Tommy that got her pregnant? And even if it was, I can't imagine him telling her to get an abortion."

Justin looked at her like she'd not understood the story. "Becky, I found them together. It wasn't hard to figure out. And Tommy gave her the money for the abortion."

"Did you talk to him about it? Ask him?"

"No. I never talked to him. I was furious. Are you not understanding that he did something destructive and it hurt other people's lives? I know he changed. And I'm ready to forgive him. But you have to be ready to accept that he wasn't perfect, Becky."

Becky took in a deep breath. She didn't want to be angry with Justin. But the things he was saying pained her to hear. And she couldn't believe Tommy wouldn't have told her about something so important. He would have. "I don't know, Justin. I know you believe that's what happened but—"

"I was there, Becky. I admire your love and devotion and belief in him. It's beautiful. I hope one day someone can love me like that. But—"

"That's enough." Becky stood, putting her hands out to stop whatever it was that he was going to say next. He was right—she hadn't been there. Tommy had not told her about this part of his life, which was harder to accept than anything else Justin was saying. Her faith in Tommy was starting to waver and she didn't like that. She was carrying his child. She needed to know that he'd been true to her and their life together. Wasn't that what a marriage was all about? Trust and truth and sharing? She needed time to absorb all that he was saying and set it back straight in her mind and her heart. "Don't taint what Tommy and I had by saying these things to me. Tommy was at peace with God. Maybe that doesn't mean anything to you, but to me it meant everything."

Justin looked up at her softly. "I wasn't telling you these things to speak ill of Tommy. That would be cruel and I could never be cruel to you."

"Then why? Why did you finally decide to tell me this?"

He stood and took her hands in his. "Because keeping it back was coming between us. I thought that once I got it out of the way, our friendship could move forward. I'm sorry, Becky. Maybe it was the wrong thing to do."

"Maybe it was." She didn't look back at him and she pulled her hands away. She didn't know what to say. She'd asked for this and now was sorry that she had. She should not have come with Justin today. In fact, she shouldn't have done anything with him. It seemed that everyone else had been right and she had been wrong. There *was* no getting around what had happened in the past. It would forever be a barrier between the two families. And, therefore, a barrier between Justin and herself. "Take me home, please."

Justin nodded and called William over.

Chapter Seventeen

After dropping off Becky and William, Justin turned up the music in his Jeep, gripped the steering wheel tighter and revved the engine, but he couldn't drown out the replay of Becky's words in his mind.

Tommy was at peace. The words screamed through his head like an F-18. Was it really possible? Had a guy like Tommy found peace with God? How? After what the man had done... While he, Justin Winters, who spent his days trying to help and save people, struggled to sleep at night.

And what about Becky? She'd lost her mother, her father, her husband and he had *seen* her unsettled at times, sad, lonely, struggling. And yet there was a certain calm to her, a kind of steadiness. He could only imagine her peace came from the Lord, in spite of her fear of loss—it was part of what made her so beautiful.

And she was beautiful. And kind, and intelligent, and he'd fallen for her like a loose anchor. Just like his mother and sister had predicted. And now he'd ruined that. He thought by telling her about the past that they could move forward but all he'd done was hurt her. She was right. What did it matter anymore? It was the past. He hated how his sister had been hurt, but he'd forgiven Tommy. Hadn't he? Or at least, thanks to Becky, he was working on it.

Justin tried to think back to all those years ago. He'd been so angry at the time he hadn't really listened to either Katie or Tommy. There had been so much to deal with over Mr. Kirkpatrick's embezzlement accusations at his father. Then Katie up and ran off. Justin had tried to be the glue that kept the family together. But it had been too much for an eighteen year old. The final blow was his father's death. By then, Justin had signed up to join the army and left home as soon as possible.

He could try going back to the army now. The panic attacks were past and he felt physically and mentally ready for combat. But emotionally? Emotionally he was still a mess. He'd be no good to his unit like this. Justin drove home and retreated to his room, trying to decide what to do.

"What's wrong?" Katie stepped up to the bedroom door.

"Nothing."

That sounded lame, but so did anything else he could think to tell her. He certainly wasn't going to tell her the truth—that because he had no peace in his heart he'd screwed things up with Becky.

Closing his closet door, he turned to face his sister, giving her a halfhearted smile. "Nothing is wrong. Just thinking about getting back to work soon. I need to get my dress blues dry-cleaned."

Katie lifted an eyebrow. "Right. That would make perfect sense, seeing as how they're hanging in your closet right now, already sealed in plastic."

Justin dropped his shoulders and let out a deep sigh. So much for hiding his distress. Katie took another step into the room and crossed her arms over her chest.

"Is this about Becky Kirkpatrick?"

Justin flinched. "This has nothing to do with Becky Kirkpatrick."

"Really? I thought maybe something happened while you were having dinner with her and flying over the countryside together." Katie wiped her cheek and looked at him like a traitor.

Was he? Was he a traitor to his sister by caring about and spending time with Becky? Justin shook away the guilt. "Holding on to your grudge against the Kirkpatricks is only hurting you, Katie. You need to let it go."

"I'm not holding on to anything. I just don't want the Kirkpatricks to be part of my life anymore. Or yours."

Justin looked away, running a hand over his short hair. And *that* was the crux of his dilemma, that he wanted Becky Kirkpatrick to be a part of his life. Something that would never be.

"Here." Katie grabbed his hand. "This card came for you."

He took the postcard, and Katie walked away.

Justin lifted the card and turned it over.

Dear Major Winters,

My husband often spoke of you as the man who kept him ready for life—since in addition to being his doctor, you often shared scriptures and attended worship together. Thank you for being with him in those last moments. Thank you for sharing his last words. We are well, Major, and at peace with Adam's death. He died trying to help a village of rebels, which we understand you were still able to tend to. It doesn't get more noble than that. We pray for your peace. May you find it in your heart,

Mrs. Adam Gentry.

Justin read and reread the message, even though the words had started to blur through the pool of tears in his eyes. *That elusive peace—how do I get it?* He hadn't found it by running. And he hadn't found it in anger. There was only one place left to go.

Justin dropped his head and began to pray.

Becky would have rather been anywhere than in the hospital clinic with Justin Winters.

"My diabetic meter quit working." She handed the device to him.

"Let me have a look." He took it from her, carefully avoiding contact with her fingers.

A month had passed since the day Justin had taken her flying. They hadn't really spoken since. A few words exchanged at church and play practices. Other than that she did her thing and he did his. She wasn't angry with him. She had wanted to know what had happened. Or rather, what he believed had happened. And he had told her. It was what she had asked for all along. What made her sad was that Justin actually thought Tommy had done those things.

Ironic how, in the end, Aggie had been right after all. She would never be friends with the Winters family. Tommy would always be between them.

Becky squirmed at the silence in the room.

"I don't usually come to the clinic," she said, looking anywhere but at him. "But since it's Saturday, Dr. Klein's office is closed. His service told me I either had to come here or drive to Nashville."

"Relax, Becky." She could feel his eyes on her. She wondered if they were full of sorrow, like they'd been that day by the river. "This is why the clinic is here. You don't need to apologize for using it. Did you try a new battery?"

She tucked a wisp of hair behind her ear. Good. He was going to be all business. That would make this easier. "Yes. I did. It still didn't work. And I went to the pharmacy to get another meter but they didn't have what I needed. They told me I should drive to Nashville, but I wasn't sure that was a good idea without checking—"

"No." The intensity of his voice made her turn to him. And the eye contact did what it always did, rendered her unable to look away. "You did the right thing coming here first. Anyway, we have some rental equipment at the hospital. If I can't get this working, I can find something for you to use until you can order a new meter. You don't need to drive to Nashville."

Justin's cool professionalism rattled Becky's nerves all the more. He started toward the door with her meter, turning it over in his hands. "Do you think you've gotten a good reading today?"

"I don't know."

"Then while you're here, we should do a blood workup. Okay?"

"Yes, sure. That's what the doctor's service said would probably happen." But not what she wanted. She wanted to get out of there.

"How have you been feeling lately?" he asked.

"Fine." *Tired.* "I can't seem to stop eating. Guess that *shows* without saying." She glanced down at her tummy, which seemed to have rounded out like a little beach ball in the last few weeks.

Justin flashed that smile of his—the one that melted her into a lump of useless putty. For a quick moment, it dissolved that barrier between them and she noticed there was something different about him. Something in his look, in his air… He seemed even more confident and sure of himself than usual.

"If by that, you mean people can actually tell you're having a baby," he teased, "then yes, you are showing a tad. It's about time, isn't it? You're what? Seven months?"

"More. Thirty-three weeks. I don't know where the time has gone." She sighed, forgetting her awkwardness for a moment. It was nice to share her thoughts with someone. With him. "It's still hard to believe it's really happening. Even seeing her little fingers and toes with all the ultrasound checks."

He leaned his hip against the counter, cocked his head to the side and looked her in the eye. A jolt of awareness sparked through her. She had missed him. Missed their conversations and walks and dinners together. She'd missed the soothing tone of his voice.

"You always call the baby a she. Is that a guess?"

The conversation felt natural. And there was the danger. She had to be careful—guard herself since they couldn't really be friends. "I wasn't going to find out. But with so many ultrasounds, it was impossible not to peek."

"So, a girl? That's great." Genuine excitement sounded in his voice. "You must be thinking about names?"

Her eyes cut away. No. She hadn't thought about names. Names scared her. If the baby had a name then she would be too real. Too close. Someone else she could lose. "No. No names. Not yet."

Justin frowned as if he detected her fear.

"I'll be right back." He left the tiny exam room, which had grown warm.

Becky stood, took off her jacket and laid it on the table, feeling silly for having rambled on about the baby. He didn't want to hear about that. And she didn't want to tell him about it, either. Just like she didn't want to tell him about her dizziness and fatigue in the last few days.

Minutes passed before Justin returned with a syringe prepped to draw blood. "Wanna push up your sleeve?"

She nodded and began to roll up her left sleeve.

He wiped her skin with antiseptic. "I've been listening in at the rehearsals. The play is really coming along."

"Yes. Next week is the big performance. I'm both excited for it and dreading it. Once it's over, so is my job. Mrs. Fox will be returning to school."

Justin concentrated on his task as he held her arm, preparing to draw blood. Becky sucked in a quick breath as he examined her arm. Good thing he wasn't checking her pulse. It was certainly racing now. Even though there wasn't anything special in the way he went about drawing the blood. He wasn't even particularly tender. The awkwardness and agitation was all hers. Justin seemed completely at ease. How was that?

Becky released a deep, slow breath as he skillfully drew her blood. He placed a bandage on her arm and backed away, disposing of the syringe, and taking up the blood sample.

"Okay. Sit tight. I'm going to test this blood and see if we can't find a meter for you that works. The one you were using is dead."

He walked to the door and paused. "Becky, just so you know, I'll be leaving after the play. Going back to my unit. I went up to Fort Campbell last week and passed my evaluations. And I've clocked up some flight hours through Mr. Gaines. Anyway, I wanted to say thanks. It wouldn't have happened without you."

He was leaving after the play. He wouldn't be there for her when the baby… Becky shook the silly thought from her head. "Me? What did I do?"

He smiled softly at her. "So much."

He locked eyes with her for a long moment. And she saw it in him again—serenity. Justin had healed. He was over his battle of nightmares and anger and fear. And he was leaving. Leaving her.

Finally, he looked away to where his hand touched the door. He turned the knob and left.

Becky stared at the door, feeling trapped inside the little room with her racing emotions. She felt dizzy and nauseous. She had to get away from that tiny room so that she could breathe. She wanted away from that clinic with Justin and the strange emotions he was causing her to feel. It was all pressing in on her and she couldn't make any sense of it. Not at all.

Justin strode away from the exam room in the direction of the lab. Becky didn't look good. She seemed tired. He'd noticed her fatigue in the past couple of days at the school play practices. From afar. He'd done a good job of keeping his distance from her in the past few weeks, as she seemed to want. But it hadn't been easy. It was the same struggle every day not to check on her, not to ask her to dinner, not to walk her out to her car. Call him pathetic. But what could he do? He found in Becky all the things he admired in a woman and more. She was strong and beautiful and loving and kind. But Becky wasn't ready for him. Maybe she never would be, not to mention all the complications of Katie and Aggie and the past between the two families. At least he'd found his own peace and let go of all that anger. Becky had had so much to do with that happening for him. He wished he could tell her about it all. Maybe one day.

Justin waited while the lab ran the quick blood test, which told him what he already suspected—that Becky's blood sugar was low. Really low. In fact, he was surprised she hadn't gone into shock. She would need a shot of insulin right away. As a courtesy, he phoned Dr. Klein's emergency number and conferred then headed to the hospital pharmacy for the insulin and a new meter and raced back to the clinic.

But he was too late. The door to Becky's exam room was open. Wide open. And Becky was gone.

Justin's heart hammered against his ribs. He rushed down the clinic corridor.

"Where's the patient from this room?" he asked the technician from triage.

The woman shrugged. Justin ran to the front desk receptionist.

"Mrs. Kirkpatrick, the pregnant woman? Tall. Gorgeous. Did you see her leave?"

"Sure. I checked her out." The young woman smiled. "About fifteen minutes ago. But don't worry—she covered her copay."

"I don't care about her copay. I didn't treat her. She could— Oh, never mind. Never mind." He put a hand to his forehead. Yelling at the receptionist wasn't going to help. But what would? Becky needed this insulin. "Did she leave a phone number?"

"Sure. A home and a cell."

"Call them both," Justin instructed as he backed away. "Tell her to stop wherever she is and wait for me."

Justin packed up some supplies along with the insulin and the new meter. He grabbed the keys to his Jeep and passed back through the reception area.

"No answer on either line," the receptionist informed him. "I left messages."

Justin swallowed hard. Where would he go to find her? *Oh, Becky, why didn't you wait?* He tried to calm his spinning head. "She probably hasn't had a chance to get home yet. Keep calling both numbers. Tell her she needs insulin immediately and to stop driving and stay wherever she is until I get there. Then call me."

"Where are you going?" she asked.

"To find her."

Justin left through the front doors and headed to his car.

Chapter Eighteen

Justin drove fast toward Becky's home. He hoped he was overreacting. But knowing that she'd passed out once due to low insulin made him think it might happen again. And it would be his fault.

He shouldn't have gone into all that personal business while she was in the exam room. He should have known it would make her nervous. She was getting ready to have a baby. She was tired and scared.

He should have told her to lie down. He should have brought her some orange juice.

She seemed sad, too. That was probably his fault, as well. She was upset over what he'd told her had happened between Tommy and Katie. And he didn't blame her one bit. She should have never had to hear that. All that was in the past. Forgiven, left at the Cross. It didn't need to be a part of their friendship. He and Katie and Aggie, all of them needed to let go. He'd thought he needed to protect Katie but he didn't. He needed to push his sister to move on with her life the same way that Becky had pushed him.

Justin held his breath as he drove along the narrow country road that led to the Kirkpatricks'. She needed this insulin. And fast. Around every corner, he expected to see her car on the side of the road. Or worse. But there was no sign of her.

What if she hadn't gone home? What if she'd decided to drive all the way to Nashville to see another doctor? If that were the case, then he was driving in the wrong direction. And Becky would be even longer without her medicine.

Justin dialed the clinic. The receptionist still had not been able to reach Becky on either line.

Please let her be safe at home.

Justin pulled his Jeep up in front of the Kirkpatricks' house. And his heart sank further as it didn't look as if anyone were home. He'd check anyway.

Scrambling up the front stairs with his bag of supplies, he rang the bell. Steps sounded behind the door. Becky answered.

"You—you're here." He dropped his shoulders and caught his breath. "You're here." *Thank You, Lord.*

"Yes. I live here." She folded her hands in front of her. She was not happy to see him. Well, he wasn't so happy, either. She'd scared him nearly to death.

"What were you thinking?" He pushed his way through the front door. "Your blood sugar is low. You need an insulin shot. And a new meter. I can't believe you just up and left the clinic."

"Please, come in." Becky watched him barge into the house, her arms still folded over her chest.

He cut his eyes back at her. Was she trying to be funny? This wasn't something to joke about. "I'm serious, Becky. Come over here and sit down. You're lucky you haven't passed out."

He reached into his bag and began to prep the syringe.

Becky didn't move. "You left the clinic to come give me an insulin shot?"

"Yes. I did. You need one. The clinic was trying to call

you to explain. You really shouldn't have left. What if you had passed out driving?"

"Oh, I guess my phone was turned off. Sorry." She closed the front door and scratched her head. "I got kind of claustrophobic in there. I had to get some air. But I am sorry you came all the way out here. I don't know what to say."

"Say 'thank you' and sit down here and take the shot." He held up the prepped syringe.

"I already took one."

"What do you mean you already took one? At the clinic?"

"No. I have one with me. For emergencies. Dr. Klein's nurse showed me how to administer it."

He couldn't believe what he was hearing. "You took the shot without a reading? What were you thinking? You could have…"

His teeth clenched. Anger and worry swirled through him. He wanted to scream at her for such stupidity. Then it dawned on him what had actually happened. Becky chose to risk her life rather than to wait for his help. That was a sobering reality for a man in love. He closed his eyes and calmed his thoughts. With a deep breath, he put the cap back on the syringe and placed it back into his bag. He pulled out the new diabetic meter he'd rented for her from the hospital, walked over to her and took a reading.

It was normal.

"Here." He placed the meter in her hands. "Use it."

"On the way home, I suddenly remembered that Aggie's friend Mrs. Burns's husband is a diabetic. I stopped by their house and did a quick reading. I don't know why I didn't think of it sooner."

"You shouldn't have left the clinic, Becky. It was reckless and dangerous. You had to have been feeling poorly and you didn't say a word to me." He started through the door.

"Wait. Justin."

He kept walking.

"I'm sorry. I overreacted. I shouldn't have left. Please, Justin. It's just that we haven't talked and now you're already going back to the army."

That was what bothered her? His leaving? He stopped in the doorway. Was it possible that she could face her feelings for him?

"Please. I'm allowed to make a mistake, okay? I'm allowed to make one lousy, stupid mistake. Please." Her voice struggled. She was crying and he knew if he turned around to face her he'd have her in his arms. And that was where she belonged.

He took in a deep breath. Did she care? Had she forgiven him for telling her about the past? That—

Her hand touched his shoulder softly. "Thank you for coming to check on me. I shouldn't have left but I—I panicked."

He knew what that was like. He turned and faced her, his heart pounding in his chest. His pulse so strong he wondered if she could feel it beating at his neck where her hand rested.

"You could have really hurt yourself, Becky." He dropped his bag of supplies to the floor, wrapped his arms around her shoulders and pulled her into his chest. "Then what would I have done?"

"I'm sorry. I'm so sorry. It's so hard to see you sometimes. And so wonderful at the same time." She leaned into the warmth of him. Tears filled the corners of her eyes and dripped down to his shirt.

"I know. I know." He kissed her hair. Her forehead. Her moist blue eyes looked up into his. "Thank God you're okay."

He wanted to cry himself. But there was something else

he wanted to do more. He slid his palms to her cheeks and watched as she closed her eyes against his touch. He leaned in and kissed her salty cheeks and then her lips. His fingers weaved in and out of her hair as she kissed him back, her hands flat against his chest. Nothing in his life had ever felt so good nor so sweet to him.

Until she pushed him away.

"I can't." She backed away.

"Becky, please. I know I hurt you when I told you about the past. But you were right. You were right about everything. I thought so much about all you've said to me. I should have listened to Tommy's side of the story. And yes, Katie was young but she wasn't naive. She went after Tommy and Tommy always kept her at arm's length. Always. So what would have changed that night? If there was a mistake made the night I left them alone, then I was wrong to blame only him. I was young and judgmental and prideful. I couldn't even consider that there was another side to things. I've spent the last few weeks doing a lot of letting go…of anger and old hurts. Forgiving people, myself included, for circumstances that may not have been in their control or in my power to change. I have a way to go, but I'm getting there."

His words and touch warmed Becky's heart. "I'm so glad to hear you say that. I didn't want Tommy to be between us. Our friendship has been too—"

Justin stepped in close to her again, taking her fingers into his hands. He held them tight, lifted them to his mouth and, one at a time, kissed each hand slowly, keeping his eyes steady on her. She should have stopped him, but he felt so strong and comforting, as if each kiss would erase away all that was between them. But she knew better. She knew she couldn't let herself slip away with her emotions.

"I've missed you these past weeks. Becky, please say we can—"

"No, Justin." She shook her head, pulling her hands back to her sides. "We can't. I've missed you, too. But I've thought over what you've said and I can't." She turned away from him and dropped her head.

"You can't what? I don't understand. There's something special between us. Are you going to deny that?"

She sighed. He was going to make this difficult. "No. I care deeply for you, but I don't want this. It isn't just the past standing between us—it's the future, too. When you told me your plans, I realized that I have to protect myself. I can't live through another loss. So I won't set myself up for it."

"Another loss? What do you mean?" He frowned deeply.

She turned back and eyed him harshly. "You're leaving, Justin. You told me you would, as soon as the play is over. You'll go back to the army."

"That's not leaving. That's my job."

"I know. And you need someone who can cope with what you do and where you go. You said so yourself. But I'm not that person. I'm sorry. I really am. But I have to focus on my health and my baby and Aggie. It's all I can do. I don't have any more to give."

Justin's teeth clenched as he fought for control of his emotions. He leaned over and gathered up his bag again. He walked back through the door. His dark eyes were angry and hurt as he turned back over his shoulder. "You have so much more to give, Becky. You're just choosing not to give it."

He walked out, slamming the door behind him.

Chapter Nineteen

Becky shut her eyes tight and leaned her forehead against the panel of the big wooden door Justin had shut. She'd done the right thing, sending him away. The two of them together made no sense.

So why did she feel so torn to pieces? Why did she want him back beside her? Holding her. His lips against her own.

"Well, I thought I had seen it all." Aggie's voice sounded from far down the long hallway. Her heels clicked against the marble flooring until she appeared at the entrance to the den. "I can't even tell you how revolted I am by that little scene. Shocked. Horrified. You know, little by little, Rebecca Rhodes, you are turning out to be exactly the kind of girl that I thought you were."

Becky spun around. "Careful, Aggie. I'm a step away from packing up, and I don't think either of us really wants that to happen."

"Then explain to me what I just saw."

"I care about Justin Winters. He's a good man. He loved Tommy. And now he wants to love me. But I told him to go. I don't want him in my life. I'm not ready for anything like that and probably never will be."

Aggie looked on, blinking. "I don't know what he told you. But he was half the reason I lost Tommy all those years ago. He's not a good man. People forget what he did."

"No, Aggie. Not forget." Anger and other emotions coated her heavy words. She was tired, so tired of Aggie's pointed finger. "They forgive. Justin knows he was wrong not to listen to Tommy's side of things. But how about you? Did you talk to Tommy? Did you stand up for him? No, Aggie. You just paid to have him sent away like you were ashamed of your own son."

Aggie looked away shamefully. "His father did that. Not me. But you're right. I did nothing to stop it. I never wanted to believe those things. Don't you understand how that made me look? Like I was a failure as a mother—"

Becky shook her head. "Don't make this about your problems, Aggie. This is about Tommy. Not that it would have changed a thing for me if he had done all of those things that Justin told me, but I know Tommy and he would have told me about them. We would have discussed it."

"So what are you saying?" Aggie looked horrified. "Are you saying the Winters family lied?"

"At first that's what I wanted to believe. But no. That's not it. And Justin is not that kind of man."

"What then?"

"Well, if Tommy didn't tell me about what happened, then I have to believe he was keeping a secret for someone." Becky watched a concerned expression wash over Aggie's face. She took a seat in the nearby den. Aggie followed and sat beside her.

"Tell me what happened after Justin found Katie and Tommy together," Becky said.

Aggie let out a deep sigh. "Oh. It was all so horrible. Remember I told you about Mr. Winters and the financial scandal at Kirkpatrick Enterprises?"

"Yes. You said that Mr. Winters embezzled funds. But that your husband didn't press charges because he died in an airplane crash."

"Right. But that's not exactly the order of things." She waved a hand through the air. "There was a deal made. Katie wouldn't press charges against Tommy—since Tommy was eighteen and she was a minor—if Tommy would leave town. And Ward wouldn't press charges against Mr. Winters but would allow him to resign."

"And Tommy agreed to that?" Becky frowned.

Aggie nodded. "He suggested it."

Becky pushed her hair back from her face, thinking about the whole story. But still nothing came together for her. What would have made Tommy come up with such an idea? Running off to boarding school? Giving a girl money for an abortion? Didn't sound at all like the man she married. The more she learned about this crazy event the less the story made sense. They were all missing something. She was sure of it. "What about the money he supposedly gave to Katie?"

"There were a few hundred dollars missing from Tommy's account about the same time my husband and I transferred him to the private school up north. A week later, Mr. Winters died in a plane crash. The next day my husband ran off with his administrative assistant. The company was turned over to my care. Just like that my family was gone."

"What happened with everyone else?"

"As you know, Tommy stayed up north for college and work. Well, until he took the job in Atlanta. Tommy's brother already lived in Europe and still does. I've been alone here ever since this happened."

"And the Winters family?"

"They had a hard time after losing their father. Mrs. Winters went back to work. Justin joined the army. Katie stayed here, as far as I know. After Tommy left, they hushed the story. I don't think anyone outside the two families knew about the pregnancy."

"And how much time are we talking about? How long from when Justin found Tommy with his sister until you sent him away?"

"Not long. A few weeks."

That didn't sound like long enough for someone to know they were pregnant. Becky kept that thought to herself. "How did you feel about all of this, Aggie?"

"How do you think I felt? I was a failure both as a mother and a wife. I quit everything when that happened. Stayed here at Greyfield. Until you came…"

Becky took Aggie's hand in hers and held it tight. "Tommy loved you, Aggie. He never thought you were a bad mother. He only worried that you weren't happy."

Tears pressed the corners of Aggie's gray eyes. "Not sure I remember how to be happy. But…I think I'd like to learn again."

Becky couldn't believe her nine weeks as a substitute teacher were coming to an end tonight at the final performance of the play. In a way, she was glad. For one, her pregnancy was nearing the end and her energy level was definitely fading. Not to mention, the less she saw of Justin the better. She did care for him, but there was no way for all the things between them to be worked out. And even if there were, she didn't have the strength to care about someone whose life was on the line most of the time. There was another woman out there for Justin Winters—one without tainted connections and a rack of fears.

Becky had also decided she would not stay in Glendale after the baby was born. She and Aggie had connected much better than she'd ever thought possible, but if she stayed longer she would wear out her welcome. Moving out would be the final step in moving forward with her life.

Becky dressed in a long flowing sundress, applied her makeup, tested her blood sugar and grabbed her purse. She slowed as she passed the bookshelves, glancing down at the four yearbooks. Tonight would be the last time she would see Justin and Katie. She thought of Tommy's letter safely tucked away inside the annual. Since talking to Justin that day in the mountains, she hadn't been tempted to read it or to throw it away, but if she were going to give it to Katie, perhaps tonight was the night.

What should I do, Lord? Let this past be buried once and for all? Or take the letter to Katie and let Tommy have his say?

Becky didn't kid herself. Even though she could hardly accept the fact that Tommy could have hurt Katie Winters, there was still a part of her that suspected the letter contained an apology of some sort. What else could it be?

Still, she reached down to the bookshelf, removed the old yearbook from the stack and opened it. She pulled out the green envelope, slid it inside her purse and headed to the school for the show.

The auditorium was packed. The house lights down. The stage bustling with students in costume.

"Places. Places," Katie whispered. The students quieted down and Justin pulled open the stage curtains.

William began his banter with the other players. Becky held her breath. Could an eleven-year-old really do this?

My nose is Gargantuan! William made a wild movement with his arms around the stage. Then he crossed his eyes to look at his nose and continued with his lines. *A great nose is the banner of a great man, a generous heart, a towering spirit, an expansive soul—such as I unmistakably am, and such as you dare not to dream of being...*

Three minutes into the show, the crowd was in his hand. He inflected the words with perfection, pausing in all the right places. Laughter filled the auditorium. By the end of the first act, the whole production was running like a well-oiled machine. Every student in place. Every line spoken with gusto. The sets sparkled under the stage lights. A few mothers had come to help with makeup and backstage management. Becky decided to take advantage and walk out to the floor to get the full effect of their hard work.

"I see you have the same idea as I do," Justin whispered to her.

A rush of warmth and longing rustled inside of her at the sound of his voice. She turned her head to him. He stood so close she could breathe in the musky scent of him.

"They are doing a wonderful job," she whispered back. "And Justin, the sets are beautiful."

"*You* are beautiful." He reached for her in the darkness of the theater. Taking her hand, he caressed it softly in his own then pressed her fingers to his lips and released it. "We should talk, Becky."

No. No talking. Her heart raced wildly at his touch. "When do you leave?"

"In a couple of days. Straight back to Afghanistan."

"That's great. That's what you wanted."

"Thanks to you. You really helped me get through this."

She smiled, shaking her head slightly. "And you helped me."

He sucked in a large breath. "Becky, I could stay. I could leave the army."

"Shhhh." She pressed a finger to his lips. "Let's just watch the play."

*   *   *

When the production was over, a reception for all the students and parents who'd helped took place in the cafeteria. One table had been set with cookies, crackers and punch. There were three large cards on top—one each for Katie, Justin and her. All the students had signed hers and written sweet goodbyes. Becky fought back her sadness. She didn't want to think of this as the end. She also couldn't think of Justin's offer to quit his work. Did he care for her that deeply? And could she accept that kind of sacrifice? She knew how much he loved his job, how important it was to him.

She sighed away the thoughts. She had one thing to do and then she could go home.

Katie had avoided her all evening, staying on one side of the stage while Becky was on the other. In fact, even though she and Justin had hardly spoken to one another in the past weeks, Katie's avoidance of her seemed to have increased. Before leaving, Becky sought her out to hand her the green envelope.

"What's this?" she asked.

"It's a letter from Tommy to you."

Katie snatched it from her. She turned the envelope over in her hands and saw where Becky had started to tear the seal.

"I thought about opening it, but I didn't. It's yours. I found it in an old yearbook a few weeks ago. I hope it brings you some peace."

Katie slipped Tommy's letter into her pocket and gave Becky a nod before walking away.

There. That was done. Now she could go home.

The Gaines family kept Justin cornered during most of the reception. Being new, they didn't know many of the other families. Also, William had told them he'd be heading back to the army soon and they thought of this as their big chance to thank him a million times for William's new medicine and for helping Mr. Gaines find so many clients.

Justin was glad he'd helped them, but it was for Becky he'd done those things. He watched her constantly from his spot in the corner. She looked fetching in the pale sundress she wore. The students hugged her and seemed sad to part with her. They weren't the only ones.

He'd waited over the past couple of weeks, waited patiently for Becky to realize they were meant to be together. It seemed so clear to him. He was willing even to quit his position as flight surgeon, so there would be nothing standing between them. And still she would have no part of him.

Lord, I don't know what to do. How much time does she need?

Becky had her bag on her shoulder, ready to leave. She stopped to speak to Katie, which made him cringe. But that didn't last long and now she was headed to the door. Justin excused himself from the Gaines family and headed toward her.

Becky smiled up at him, but she looked upset. He hoped Katie hadn't been the cause.

"Can I walk you out?" he offered.

She nodded.

"You didn't let me finish what I was saying earlier." He offered her an arm and led her toward the teacher parking lot.

"You were meant to be a flight surgeon, Justin. I would never ask you to give that up."

"You didn't ask. I'm offering."

She shook her head. "It wouldn't matter. I'm just not ready."

"Then I'll wait."

"I'm going back to Atlanta," she said. "Once the baby is born."

"I think that's a mistake, Becky. Stay here." He grabbed her hand and squeezed it again. "Raise your little girl here. With me."

She frowned. "I can't, Justin. You need to accept that. There's someone else out there for you. Someone with less baggage."

They walked on in silence until they reached her car. He struggled for words from his breaking heart.

She pulled her keys out and turned to him. "Well, I guess this is goodbye."

"It doesn't have to be," he said.

"I think it's what's best."

The idea came to him. Use her words. "No, it's what's safe."

"What?"

"Becky, you dole out all that advice about moving on and putting the past behind, but you don't follow it."

"Excuse me?" Her eyes were wide with surprise.

"You're moving back to Atlanta because it's safe," he told her.

Her face reddened. "No. I'm moving to Atlanta because that *is* moving on with my life. I can't stay here and hide away with Aggie forever."

"That's not what you're doing at all." He took a step back. "You're leaving because you're afraid. You're afraid of getting hurt. Afraid of loving anyone and losing them like you did your mother or Tommy. It's like you think if you're not here you can quit caring. That's why you haven't named the baby. A name would make her too close. And you're leaving Glendale because you've started to care too much about Aggie. And we both know how you feel about me. But

Becky, there's no way to protect yourself from getting hurt in life. You of all people should know that."

Her eyes darkened with anger. That was okay, though. At least she was listening.

"That's ridiculous," she said.

"Is it? Have you named the baby?"

"No."

He glared back at her.

"Oh, Justin, that proves nothing. Lots of people wait until the baby is born to name it."

"Have you bought things for the baby? Found a pediatrician?"

"Aggie's d-done some shopping," she stammered. "I haven't had time. I will. I still have a few weeks left."

He tilted his head and folded his arms over his chest.

"Stop this, Justin. Maybe I just don't feel for you the way you feel about me."

She was weakening. *Good.* He stepped in, lowered his head to hers, his hands on her shoulders, and kissed her hard. Kissed her through her tears.

Then he stepped back and caught his breath. "You do, Becky Kirkpatrick. You love me. I know that you do."

He turned away and walked back inside the school.

Chapter Twenty

Justin didn't know what he had expected by talking to Becky, but he'd expected something. He started throwing his clothes into his duffel with force.

She loved him. He knew she did. Even if she wouldn't admit it.

He tossed in a few sets of scrubs.

But what if she never could get over her fears? Or never get past loving Tommy enough to love him, too.

He continued to pack his belongings. He was to leave in the morning. It was what he had to do. But he would be leaving his heart here. Or Atlanta. Or wherever she'd be.

A soft rap sounded at his bedroom door.

"Come in."

Katie pushed the door ajar. She looked horrible, standing there looking almost catatonic, her makeup smudged under her eyes and her hair unkempt.

"Katie, what's the matter?"

She walked in and handed Justin a handwritten note. He took it from her and began to read.

Dear Katie,
Don't worry about Justin thinking that we slept

together. He'll realize sooner or later that I would never do that. You're like a sister to me. So I shouldn't have kissed you, either. That was stupid. But you asked me to, so I did. Anyway, I'm going to go away for a while because I can't be here and not tell the truth. And no, I'm not talking about what people think of you and me. I already have a terrible reputation thanks to Kimberly Lipscomp. Wow. Talk about bad mistakes.

No. I'm talking about our fathers. I overheard my dad on the phone with someone. I guess it was a lady because he said he couldn't wait to—well, never mind that part. The important part is that I heard him say your dad didn't embezzle the funds from Kirkpatrick Enterprises, but that he was going to charge him anyway because he didn't want to go to jail himself. Actually, it kind of sounded like my dad took the money. Which makes me sick. I wish there was someone else I could tell, but who would believe me? And how could I prove it? So here's the deal—my dad will drop the charges against your father if your dad resigns. It's better than your family fighting Kirkpatrick Enterprises in court. The bad part is that my dad's sending me away so I don't rat him out.

Not for long, I hope. Anyway, I hope you got the money you asked for. Yeah, I got money out of the deal, too. That was to not tell my mother. Like I would have anyway. She'd have been crushed. Okay, I got to go pack now. I'll miss you. And Justin. Maybe once this blows over we can all hang out again.
Your friend, Tommy

Justin handed the letter back to his sister. She took it from him slowly as if waiting for his wrath to explode against her.

"How long have you had that letter?" he asked, trying to keep his voice steady.

"Becky found it in an old yearbook. She gave it to me tonight after the play. I had no idea."

"You had no idea what? Katie, you let us all believe horrible things about Tommy. Why?"

"I don't know. I was pregnant. I was scared. I guess I thought it sounded so much better to have been with Tommy than with…"

"Brad. You had dated Brad right before that."

"Yes. He's the one who told me to get an abortion and not to tell anyone or he would break up with me. I was fifteen. I was so stupid."

"Tommy didn't know what that money was for, did he?"

"No, he didn't. I just told him I needed money and he left it for me. I don't think he ever knew about the abortion, unless his mother told him."

"You used him, Katie. You used Tommy. Why didn't you tell us the truth?"

"I told Dad. And then the crash."

"But after that, Katie?"

"I don't know. You ran off to the army. And Tommy never came home, so I thought what does it matter? Then Becky came, and I didn't want either one of us anywhere near her, because she made me think about a part of my life I didn't want to remember. I'm sorry. More so than you can ever imagine."

Justin picked up his baseball cap from the bed and threw it across the room. "Well, you got your wish. She wants nothing more to do with me. So now what?" Justin was angry. Mostly angry with himself for not having had more faith in his best friend. Becky had been right all along.

"There's still time to fix this," Katie said. "I never settled things with Tommy because I thought he just left. I didn't know his father made him leave. And now it's too late for me to say I'm sorry to him. But I have to make this right somehow for you." Tears poured down her cheeks. "I'm so sorry, Justin. So sorry. Tell me what to do. I want to fix this. I know you love her."

Justin dropped his head for a moment, trying to control his emotions. He looked at his sister, ready to start in on how many ways she'd hurt him and others by not speaking up. Then again, he'd hurt her, too. Run off to the army when she'd needed him. That's why she'd been upset with Tommy—not because he took advantage of her, but because he left her, left town, right when she needed his friendship and support. And he had done the same thing.

Katie was sobbing now. She collapsed onto his bed, holding the letter to her chest. Justin could still see a scared little fifteen-year-old who'd made a bunch of bad decisions and didn't know where to turn.

He sat down beside her and ran a hand through her dark hair.

"Do you hate me?" she asked.

Justin shook his head. "Nope. Do you hate me for leaving?"

She lifted her head to look his way. "No, Justin, I never hated you for anything. Do you think you can forgive me for keeping that secret?"

He nodded. "Already done."

"I didn't know what Tommy had done for our father."

"I guess no one did. But it totally fits, doesn't it? Sounds just like him."

"Yes, it does." Katie sat up and faced him. "Do you think it's too late for you and Becky?"

"I hope not, Katie. I sure hope not."

* * *

"Here's your dinner." Aggie entered Becky's room carrying a tray loaded with soup, salad and crackers.

"Thank you, Aggie." Becky pushed herself to the edge of the bed.

Aggie placed the tray on the table beside her and started for the door.

"Will you stay?" Becky asked. "It gets a little dull being in here all day and night."

Aggie turned and smiled. "You've only been on bed rest for two days." She walked back into the room and sat in an armchair near the bed.

"I know, and you can't imagine how slowly the time passes. I've already watched three movies and read two novels."

"How are you feeling?"

"Fine. And I wish I could convince Dr. Klein of that. I think what happened the day after the play was a fluke."

"Becky, you showed signs of premature labor. That's not a fluke. It's common with gestational diabetes, and you'd better not take chances. Look how far you've made it and staying so active. I'm very proud of you."

"You are?"

"Yes. You've faced a lot in the last year and you've done it all with grace and your head held high. I don't know why it took me so long to see what Tommy did."

Becky smiled at Aggie's sweet words. They were comforting. But what she really wanted was one of her long chats with Justin. She wondered if he'd already left for the Middle East.

She poked at her dinner. "How was church today?"

"Church itself was fine. But that garden club is a disaster. I don't know how they get anything accomplished. No one in there knows a rose from a dandelion."

Becky held back a snicker. "I'm sure they appreciate your expertise."

"I should have never stopped going…." Aggie's words were soft and full of regret.

"You're going now. That what matters."

Aggie tilted her head, studying Becky as if she weren't sure she wanted to continue the conversation. "I wasn't a good mother to Tommy and his older brother. They grew up without rules or discipline. And their father was no role model. But I should have shown them the way. Instead of losing my own."

Becky pushed away the tray of food. Finally, after all these months, after all her prayers, Aggie wanted to talk about her faith. She wasn't going to miss a minute of it. "That wasn't God's plan. Tommy found God a different way. But that's okay. So how about you?"

A few tears banked on the rims of Aggie's eyes. She nodded and wiped them away. "Well, thanks to you and Tommy, I have my faith again."

"I've prayed for that for a long, long time," she said.

"Becky, I hope you know that my home is yours for as long as you want it."

Becky felt the tears pooling in her own eyes. "It's funny you should say that. I was planning to go back to Atlanta and, well, I had a conversation with Justin after the play and since then I've been thinking maybe that's not the best idea." Justin had been right. She was running, not wanting to care about Aggie. But she did. She cared about Justin, too. She loved him. Even if it scared the daylights out of her. She loved him. Running to Atlanta wouldn't make that any less frightening. But was it too soon to love another? What would Aggie think?

"Speaking of Dr. Winters, I saw him and his sister

at church today." Aggie smiled. "We all had a very nice chat."

"You did? Really? How?" Becky tried to picture them speaking civilly to one another. She couldn't. "I thought Justin left for Fort Campbell?"

"Apparently his deployment has been postponed for several weeks, as they've asked him to work with a group of pilots in training at Fort Campbell."

"Oh." Becky tried to look indifferent. Aggie was watching her carefully. But inside she was thrilled. If Justin were that close then maybe she could see him again.

"I would have thought you'd have more to say about that," Aggie said.

"Why would I care—"

"You don't have to pretend you don't have feelings for him."

"But I don—"

"You do," Aggie interrupted again. "You're young, Rebecca. And smart and beautiful. You should share your life with someone. Someone who loves you like Tommy did. That's what Tommy would have wanted."

"This seems awkward to discuss with you. Really, Aggie, it's way too soon to even think such a thing. I don't know that I'll go down that road again. And if I do, it certainly won't be with Justin Winters."

"Whatever you say. I won't bring it up again." Aggie leaned over the tray and gave Becky a kiss on the head.

"Good. Don't. That would be great."

"Then I won't mention that he came to visit you today after church, either."

"He did? He came to see me?"

Aggie nodded. "I can see how uninterested you are in that news, as well. Good thing you were asleep so you didn't have to see him."

"Right. Although bed rest is pretty boring and—oowie," Becky gasped. She pushed away the tray and bent into a ball as a sharp contraction gripped her belly.

"What's the matter?"

"It's happening again, Aggie. The contractions."

"Oh, dear, child. Let me go call the doctor."

"Aggie." Becky grabbed her hand so that she couldn't dash off. "I'm scared."

"Every mother is scared," she whispered. "Let me call Dr. Klein. I'll be right back."

"Aggie." She turned in the doorway. "Will you call Justin, too?"

Chapter Twenty-One

"The contractions are strong and close together and her blood pressure is over the roof." Justin spoke as calmly as he could over the phone to Dr. Klein. Aggie and Becky were watching him from the next room. Both looked frightened and worried. He didn't want them to see how concerned he actually was.

"Okay, son, calm down," the doctor said over the phone line. "What is her BP?"

"One eighty over one ten."

"Okay. Take it again. Keep taking it. If it goes higher, give her a shot of hydralazine. Do you have that?"

"I do. I can do that." Justin felt a twinge of relief. He could do something to help. "And then you'll meet us at the hospital?"

"No. Becky is only thirty-four weeks. There are no preterm experts in Glendale. We need to delay the delivery. You have to get her to the NICU center in Nashville."

Nashville? That was over an hour away. And Becky was in so much pain. Justin wished he remembered more of his labor and delivery rotation from medical school. But that had been so long ago. Besides, Becky needed neonatal specialists standing by.

"What are we up against?" Justin tried not to reveal the panicked choking of his breath.

"The baby will probably be fine," assured Dr. Klein. "But it would be better to have her born where the specialists are available if she needs them. You don't want to move a preemie from one hospital to another if you don't have to."

"So we need to get Becky to Nashville before this baby is born." He hoped an ambulance could do that.

"The ambulance is en route," said Dr. Klein. "Stay calm. Give her a shot of magnesium sulfate to slow the contractions. I gave her some when she came in the other day. And keep her on her left side. I'll meet you in Nashville."

"Right. Got it." Good grief. The doctor was talking to him the way he talked to his own patients. Telling him things he already knew. And he needed it. He needed to calm down. He was a wreck. To help Becky and her baby, he needed to slow down, calm down and take charge.

He turned and faced Becky and Aggie. "Magnesium sulfate. Dr. Klein said you have some?"

"I'll get it," Aggie said, and flew from the room.

"Thank you for coming." Becky reached out a hand to him.

"I'm glad I was nearby and not back at Fort Campbell." He had stayed in Glendale hoping to visit her before driving back for the week. He smiled and patted her shoulder. Then he reached for his cuff to take her blood pressure again.

"What did Dr. Klein say?"

"Well, the good news is the ambulance is on the way." Her blood pressure was even higher. He knew her chest must feel tight, making it hard for her to breathe. Not a good thing when one was in labor and needed oxygen more than ever.

"The bad news?" She looked up at him, eyes searching for some bit of comfort.

"You need to go all the way to Nashville."

"To the NICU. I was afraid of that." She grabbed Justin's hand and squeezed it hard as a contraction passed.

"I know, Becky. It's not going to be very comfortable for you. But the magnesium sulfate should slow down the contractions. And Dr. Klein feels confident that you will make it there in time. He's already on his way." Justin stepped back to his medic bag, fumbling for the syringe of blood pressure stabilizer.

"Fly me there. Please. Fly me to Nashville, Justin. Otherwise I don't think I'll make it."

"Fly you?" He stepped beside her again and prepped the hydralazine.

"Yes. It has to be faster than driving."

"Well, it would be faster. The hangar is only five minutes from here and… But the plane may not be ready and Mr. Gaines—"

"I don't want Mr. Gaines to fly me. I want you to do it."

"Becky, it's at night and the last time I flew at night things didn't go so well."

"There won't be any land mines in Nashville. Please, Justin."

The look in her eyes would have made him fly to the moon if he knew a way to try it. "I'll call Mr. Gaines."

Aggie returned with the magnesium sulfate. Justin administered the medicine and called Mr. Gaines. William's father wasn't at the hangar, but the plane was ready and Mr. Hudgins, who also kept a plane in the same hangar, was on site and could prep the Cessna for their flight.

Panic surged through Justin's veins. Dare he fly again at night with a hurting, time-sensitive patient on board? One he was desperately in love with. And yet how could he not?

He put his phone away and walked back into the bedroom where Becky lay. The paramedic crew had arrived. They were getting ready to move her.

Lord. I want very much to have this woman by my side. She makes me want to be a better man, as do You, Lord. Help me conquer this fear.

The prayer on his lips, Justin smiled down at her. She lay, quietly fighting her pain and contractions. And her fear. She knew what they were up against. She knew her baby needed to be inside that hospital before she was born. And if she could fight her fears, then he could fight his.

"You're taking her to the Glendale airfield," he said to the paramedics.

Aggie gasped.

"It's okay, Aggie. Justin's going to fly us there."

"There's only room for four people. So it will be you, Mr. Hudgins, one of the crew and me."

Aggie nodded her understanding. "I'll get in the car now and meet you there."

Becky closed her eyes, her face scrunching tight against the contraction. "I'm glad you're here, Justin."

"There's nowhere on earth I'd rather be." Justin closed his eyes against her soft words. Never had it felt so good to be needed. He leaned in quickly and kissed her forehead. "Now, stop talking and save your strength."

The paramedics, Matt and Samantha, pushed the gurney out through the house and into the van. Justin climbed in and sat next to Becky. They reached the airfield in less than five minutes and drove straight out to the tarmac. Mr. Hudgins was waiting with the Cessna.

"Twenty minutes from takeoff to touchdown." He hurried them onto the airplane.

The paramedics helped Becky into her seat.

Samantha grabbed a small bag of supplies and climbed in next. "It would be better if she could lie down."

Mr. Hudgins jumped out of the way. "Well, I don't need to go along."

"Okay," Matt said, practically pushing Justin into the plane. "The Nashville hospital has an emergency vehicle waiting as close by as possible. Good luck."

Justin climbed in and looked at Becky. Samantha was helping her to lie down across the backseats. Did she really trust him to fly her to Nashville?

"Don't leave me." Becky's smile was skewed by her pain.

Leave it to Becky to push him past his last fear. He nodded to her. He could do this for her. He turned and prepared for takeoff.

Samantha patted Becky's arm in a motherly fashion. "Don't you worry, Mrs. Kirkpatrick. I've slowed down more labors that I can count on my fingers and toes."

Justin accelerated down the runway, feeling calm and in control. He didn't think of bombs. He didn't see Gentry's blood. He didn't worry about what to do; it all came to him naturally, his head calm and steady. His peace from the Lord. And his heart with Becky and her child. Now, to get her to Nashville without her thinking about the pain.

"So, it's probably about time you came up with a name, huh?" he yelled back to her.

"Oh, you're right," she said. "I should have listened to you and thought more about it."

"We'll think about it right now," he said. "Talk through it."

She paused to get through a contraction. "Well, I don't want anything trendy like Mackenzie or Brittney."

"How about a family name?" Samantha suggested. "Or a name with some meaning?"

"I like that idea," Justin said. "Something to remember Tommy or honor your mother by?"

"I'd love for her to have Tommy's initials. It's something they could share."

"Okay, then. A name that starts with *T*." Justin glanced back at her. She probably wouldn't remember much of this conversation, but it was helping to get her mind off her fears.

He started listing names. "Theresa. Tamela. Toni. Tiffany. Tabitha. Terry. Tori. Taylor…"

"No. They're all good names, but I don't know." Becky sighed. "Why is this so hard for me?"

Samantha monitored her blood pressure and counted contractions while they continued to discuss names.

"Maybe I'll just name her Sarah after my mother."

"That's pretty. And biblical," Justin said.

"And boring. My mother never liked her name much. That's a terrible idea."

Justin held back a snicker at Becky's worry and indecision, so glad that her mind was occupied on anything besides giving birth. Here he was worried about landing a plane? This woman was getting ready to have a baby. Nothing could be more frightening than that.

And wonderful. He looked back at her again. He was hopelessly in love.

It wasn't long before Nashville's skyline came into view and Justin located the landing strip. He could even see the ambulance waiting to the side. He steadied the small plane and touched her down, safe and sound. *Thank You, Lord.*

The hospital paramedics took over as soon as the door of the Cessna was opened. They rushed Becky out and into the small vehicle. Justin followed, holding Becky's hand as they moved her along.

"Are you the husband?" the paramedic asked.

"No," Justin said, thinking that was something he hoped to change in the near future.

"He can come," Becky said, her voice sounding more and more exhausted with every word. "He's my friend."

Her friend? He wanted to be so much more.

"Sorry," the nurse said. "No one but family allowed. You'll have to meet her at the hospital."

"But—" Becky started to protest. A contraction stopped her.

"It's okay, Becky." Justin grabbed her hand one last time, giving it a hard squeeze. "I'll see you and little Tara as soon as I can."

"Tara?"

"Well…yes. If you like that name? *T* for Tommy and also something of your mother, Sarah."

"Tara." Becky's eyes filled with tears. "It's perfect."

Justin released her hand and watched the ambulance race off to the hospital.

Chapter Twenty-Two

"I can't believe we're finally going to be home. After a whole month in the hospital. Tara is finally ready." Becky looked gratefully at Aggie, who had helped her rent an apartment in Nashville so that she could stay near the baby without the long drive each day. "Thanks for picking us up."

"I'm just glad you're coming back to Greyfield with Tara. It will be much easier to get to know my granddaughter if she's right under my nose."

"I'm glad to hear you say that, Aggie. Thank you."

"You stay as long as you want, Rebecca. In fact, I've been meaning to tell you that I heard a rumor about Mrs. Fox."

"The woman I substituted for?"

"Yes. It seems she doesn't want to work anymore. So there will be an opening at the middle school for a new teacher, you know. And I could keep Tara while you're at work."

"I thought you didn't approve of mothers working?" Becky teased.

"Well, I never said such a thing. I said Kirkpatrick women didn't work. And they didn't. Until Tommy married you."

"And that changed a few things?"

"All for the good, my dear. All for the good." Aggie smiled, then looked pensive. "I wonder what Tara will do when she's grown? We'll have to make sure she has many opportunities. I want her to have plenty of choices."

As they drove home, Aggie listed things that Tara needed and Becky tried to listen without nodding off, as had become her new M.O. since becoming a mother. She'd been dreaming of her first night's sleep in a comfortable bed with Tara in a bassinet beside her for the first time. She couldn't wait.

"Oh, look, Tara," Becky said to the sleeping baby in the car seat beside her. "Here's your home. This is Greyfield."

Aggie turned the car into the long driveway and headed to the front of the house. Even at this distance, Becky could see several cars in front and a line of people at the door.

"What's going on?"

"A little welcome home for you and Tara, of course."

"This is wonderful. Look. There's Mrs. Fitzwilliams's car. And Katie's. And Justin…"

Justin waited at the top of the drive, dressed in his camouflage fatigues. Becky's heart plummeted. She knew what that meant. It meant he was leaving. And the thought of losing him made her almost retch. It didn't matter whether you told someone you loved them or not. If they were a part of you, there was always the possibility to lose them. But it seemed as if the risk was greater with Justin working in the Middle East. And still she knew that's where he belonged. It was her own fears that stood in the way of telling Justin the truth. Could she manage them? Was she willing to try? Did Justin even want that anymore?

He'd come to see them every chance he could at the hospital, both Tara and her. But he hadn't spoken of a future with her again. Not since the night of the play. Not since the night everyone learned the truth about Tommy. For that, she was so glad. So glad Tommy had left Katie his letter. And that Katie had come forward with the truth. Katie, too, had come to visit her and the baby. The relationship wasn't completely healed but it was on its way and Becky was glad for that, as well.

But that night at the play seemed so long ago.

Aggie pulled the car to a stop and looked over her shoulder at Becky. "Well, go on. Get out. Take Tara with you."

Becky scooped Tara into her arms, wrapped her tightly in a soft fleece blanket and climbed out with the infant clutched to her chest.

"Welcome home," Justin said, revealing the most enormous bouquet of red roses Becky had ever seen.

"You're leaving," she said. "I—I don't know what to say. I knew this would happen but I—"

He smiled and kissed her cheek and then the baby's forehead. "To start with you can say thank-you for the flowers and then you can show off your beautiful baby to all these people who came here to see you. All these people love you, Becky."

Becky looked around the front lawn at all the friends. One by one, she hugged them. Some of them held the baby. Others peeked. Becky was overwhelmed. And this was no postpartum wave of hormones rushing through her. This was the realization that she'd come to Glendale knowing no one but Aggie and the Lord had provided her with a host of family-like friends.

Slowly the party moved inside the house and Tara began to fuss a bit. Dyanna approached, asking if she could take Tara to her new bassinet. Getting little Tara somewhere quiet sounded like a great idea. As she handed the baby over, Justin swept up behind them.

"Can I hold her?" he asked timidly.

Becky nodded and Justin reached out for Tara. She looked like a miniature porcelain doll in his large hands. But he held her in the manner he did all things, with gentle strength.

"I can't believe I'm finally getting to hold her. All this

time waiting and praying and hoping." He stopped and looked up at Becky. "I sound like an old lady, don't I?"

"She likes you. She stopped fussing," Becky said. "Maybe she knows you're the one who rescued her the day she was born?"

"No. That would have been the doctors at the hospital," Justin said. "All I did—"

"All you did was fly us to Nashville, where she was born twenty minutes later. Nice and safely delivered in the NICU where she needed special care to be able to breathe. She wouldn't have made it if you hadn't done that."

Justin's eyes misted a little. He handed Tara to Dyanna. "Take a walk with me?" he asked Becky.

Becky nodded and the two of them slipped away from the crowd and headed down the lane of roses toward the old chestnut tree.

"When do you leave?" she asked.

"Tomorrow."

Her heart sank all over again. She didn't want to think about life without Justin. "For Afghanistan?"

"Well, first we meet at Fort Campbell. Then, yes, we have a mission in the Middle East. Probably Afghanistan. But... there's something I wanted to talk to you about, Becky."

She looked up at him. This conversation made her nervous. She wanted Justin in her life, but it had been so long since he'd spoken of it that she guessed it was too late. And now he was leaving her. "About your going away?"

"Well, sort of." He sighed and looked away, frustrated.

They walked along a little farther from the house until they stood under the chestnut tree. Justin searched along the trunk.

"Look here." He pointed to a spot where the bark had been peeled off.

"This tree belongs to Tommy and Justin." Becky ran her

fingers over the rough carving, a little moisture forming to her eyes.

"We did that when we were twelve. Almost twenty years ago."

"And now this tree will belong to Tara."

"She's beautiful, Becky. You and Tommy made a beautiful baby girl."

Becky glanced around at the tree. Her eyes followed along the strong trunk and out to the longest branch where a bit of rope remained from what had been a tire swing. "Tommy would have made her a new one."

Justin moved in close. He placed a finger under her chin and lifted her face up. A single tear slid from her cheek and he wiped it away with his thumb. "He would have. And I'd be honored if you'd let me do that one day when Tara is ready for a swing."

"That would be nice. If you're around…" She tried to look away. She had to distance herself from him. She had only wanted to be friends with him and suddenly she felt so much more. When had that happened?

Justin gently brought her gaze back to his with another touch to her cheek. His dark eyes swallowed her up with their softness and weakened her tough resolve. "I'll be around, Becky. That's what I'd like anyway. I know no one can ever replace Tommy in your heart, but…do you think you could make some space in there for me?"

"Of course there's room in there for you. We've always been friends, haven't we?"

"No. Well, yes, we're friends, but…" He shifted his weight. "I want to be more."

She shook her head in disbelief. Could it be true? That Justin still loved her? He still wanted a life with her?

Justin frowned. "I'm sorry. I'm not very good at this." He reached into his pocket and pulled out a ring of white gold with a single diamond solitaire. "I know you're not ready to make a commitment or anything. But I thought maybe you could wear this and think about it while I'm gone. I won't be away for long. I don't ever want to be away from you for long."

Becky continued to shake her head, emotions swirling so quickly around her they stole her breath and her words. Tears started to flow.

"I love you, Becky," he continued. "I can't imagine my life without you. But I'm…" His shoulders dropped. "I'm wasting my time, aren't I?"

"No, Justin, not at all," Becky broke in, finally managing to find her voice. "I love you, too. For so long I thought that if I cared for you it meant I'd lose you. But now I know that love is worth the risk. Loving Tara. Loving Glendale. Loving Tommy. Loving you."

He reached down and pulled her hands into his, lifted them, pressing her fingers to his lips. "Will you do me the honor of becoming my wife?"

"I will," she answered. "As soon as you get back from Afghanistan."

"And you won't worry about me being away? Because if you will, I can retire and start a practice here."

"No, Justin. I'll worry. And I'll miss you. But I wouldn't change one thing about you or about the things that you do."

Justin leaned in to her and kissed her softly, sealing the promise they had made together.

Epilogue

Two years later

"Now, Mommy. Now." Tara's chubby fingers grabbed at Becky's skirts, pulling her toward the office, the computer and everyone's favorite moment of the week.

"You're right, Tara. It's time." Becky followed the precocious toddler into the office and flipped open the laptop. Catching a glimpse of her reflection in the dark monitor caused her to cringe. She could at least look decent for the satellite chat, especially today with such important news to deliver. Becky situated Tara in front of the camera and readied the computer. "Okay, sweetie. It's all ready. We'll just wait for the call."

"Tay-wah talk now." Tara stared into the computer with excited anticipation.

"Almost, baby girl. Hold on just a second." Becky took in a deep breath, scanning the room for anything that might aid her in looking a little more presentable to the man she loved. Tara might be small, but her big energy and endless curiosity made putting on makeup and combing her own hair acts of luxury. Some days Becky was fortunate to squeeze in the time for a morning shower; other days even that got put on hold until naptime or later.

Becky spotted a doll-size brush on the floor. "This will work," she mumbled to herself, grabbing the toy from the ground. She turned to a large framed photo and made out her reflection in the glass. With the tiny brush, she smoothed the ends of her big curls.

"Mommy. Pwetty." Tara tugged again at the back of her skirt as Becky straightened her blouse and pinched some color to her pale cheeks.

Not too completely awful, she decided with one last look, then turned around to click on the satellite connection now ringing through her computer. Her heart raced with anticipation. She couldn't wait to see Justin. Even though it would be for only two or three minutes, she would cherish the moments and replay it in her mind until the next time.

With an electronic whoop and loud popping sound, Justin's image appeared, live and active on the screen in front of them. Becky soaked in the comfort brought from the look in his soft, dark eyes and the wonderfully crooked curve of his smile that she'd come to know so well. She reined in the strong wave of emotions that flowed over her at the sight of him.

"Daddie!" Tara bounced in the chair, waving madly and giggling with joy.

"Hi, baby girl! Look how big you are!" He smiled, sitting calmly in front of the army computer, beaming at the little girl who'd called him daddy ever since she started talking, even though she knew she had another. "Are you taking good care of Mommy while I'm away?"

Tara nodded with wide eyes, answering yes to all his questions. Becky allowed them a full minute and then could stand it no longer. Sweeping Tara into her lap, she joined her little girl in front of the computer. If she could have, she would have gotten closer. How she longed to reach out and feel the warmth of his cheek against her palm or run her fingers through his short, dark hair.

"Now, there's the beautiful Mommy," Justin said as Becky

floated into the image captured by the tiny computer camera. "How's my new bride?"

"I'm fine." Becky chuckled at the word new. They'd been married a year now. "How's the unit?"

"We're good. Everyone is healthy. Not much work for a doctor these days."

"Good. Keep it that way. I want you back safe and in one piece."

"Affirmative. How's Aggie these days?" he asked.

"Well, besides spoiling Tara while I'm at work, she's running the garden club at church and last week started hosting a Bible study at her house. I think your mom is leading it."

"I'll bet Mom loves that. And getting to see baby girl there."

Tara nodded and clapped her hands together.

"Yeah, your mom is great. But your sister! She's the most indulgent aunt ever. Right, Tara? Aunt Katie?" Becky gave the blonde girl a kiss to the top of the head.

"Aunt K-K. Aunt K-K!" Tara wiggled out of Becky's arms and ran down the hallway in a whirl of excitement. Probably looking for Justin's sister.

"She does have Tommy's energy." Justin laughed.

"That she does." Becky smiled.

"But her mother's beauty." Justin sighed. "I miss you, Becky."

"I miss you back." Becky swallowed hard. Although his smile was pure, she could see the fatigue in him, from hours of hard work and probably sleepless days out on a mission. She longed to take him in her arms and hold him while he rested. She hoped that would be soon. "So when will you be home?"

"Thanksgiving. We'll be home for Thanksgiving. Just got the news last night."

"I'll start counting down the days."

"Sixty-two. I already looked," Justin teased. "And they'l

o by fast. They're moving us for an assignment. I don't have
he details."

I don't have the details. That was Justin's way of saying
hat he couldn't tell her what he was doing, where he was
going or when he'd be in touch again. For her, the sixty-two
days would be long. But she would give him some great in-
entive to get back home. "Well, then…I guess I'd better tell
ou the news now."

"News? What news?" He eyed her suspiciously.

Becky gave him a coy smile but said nothing.

Justin watched her in silence, tilting his head skeptically
o the side. After a long moment, a hesitant grin played with
is mouth. "This wouldn't have something to do with my
aving been home just over a month ago?"

Becky chuckled as Justin worked out the calculation
y counting weeks on his fingers. Finally he threw up his
ands.

"So, are you going to tell me or what?"

For a moment Becky wished he were there so they could
elebrate this wonderful news together. But they couldn't.
And at least she got to see his face as she told him. What a
lessing that was to her. "Yes, Justin. We have another Win-
rs on the way. A spring baby."

"That's not just news, Becky. That is the blessing of a
ream coming true." There was a sense of pride and satis-
action in his words and Becky couldn't stop the tear from
liding down her cheek.

"The blessing of family," Becky said, remembering a time
ot so long ago when that seemed like something entirely
ut of her grasp.

Now, with God's help, it was hers.

* * * * *

Dear Reader,

Thank you for picking up my first Love Inspired novel. Afte[r]
writing two suspense stories, I got the idea for Becky an[d]
Justin's story and my first contemporary romance was bor[n]
I hope you enjoyed it. I had a great time writing it.

Becky's character was a real challenge for me. I'm par[t]
of a large blended family who is such a support to me, I ha[d]
a hard time imagining what it would be like without the[m]
In fact, my favorite part of the novel (beside the romance[)]
was playing with the relationship between Aggie and Beck[y]
letting the awkwardness between them dissolve and havin[g]
the characters work toward a solid friendship.

And as this is my first complete novel since strugglin[g]
with a serious illness two years ago, I'd like to take thi[s]
opportunity to thank the editors at Love Inspired and m[y]
family for all the support. I couldn't do it without them.

In His love,
Kit Wilkinson

Questions for Discussion

1. Who do you think of when you think of family? Are these the people you turn to in times of trouble? Have they ever failed you?

2. Have you ever loved a person or a situation so much that you lived in fear of losing them/it? How did you overcome that?

3. What is your favorite scene in the story? Why?

4. Which character do you most relate to? Why?

5. If you found yourself in Becky's shoes, do you think you would have done what she did (moving in with her unfriendly mother-in-law) or would you have been more tempted to stay with friends you felt comfortable with?

6. What are some of the things Aggie does to alienate Becky? Why do you think Aggie is so bitter toward her for most of the story?

7. What are some of the reasons Becky decides to stay with Aggie at the beginning of the story? What things does Aggie do that make Becky's reasons for staying change?

8. Justin was wrong about Tommy, believing all those years that his friend had betrayed him when Tommy really had loved him sacrificially. Have you ever misjudged a person for the worse (or better)? If so, how did you feel when you learned the truth?

9. Katie was abandoned by her boyfriend Brad. She thought Tommy had abandoned her and even felt that her brother had left her behind when he joined the army. How do you think this affects Katie's relationships? Do you think Katie and Becky will become friends? Why or why not?

10. God always provides for us even if not exactly in the way we expect. Think of a time when you had a need that was cared for in an unexpected way.

11. How did you feel about the ending of the story with Justin returning to the army and being away from Becky? Was this a totally satisfying end or did it seem less happy that they were apart?

12. Justin and Becky are both struggling with fear. But Justin overcomes his by attacking them head-on. How is Becky's recovery different? Why do you think it takes her so much longer to deal with her issues?

13. How did you feel about Tommy before reading the letter that he wrote to Katie? How did you feel about Katie? Did the letter make you change your opinion of them? How about your opinions of Becky and Justin? How did the revealing letter change your opinion of them (if at all)?

14. One of my favorite stories in the Bible is the one of Ruth and Naomi, and it's where I got the idea for this story. Discuss the similarities and differences of the relationships between Ruth and Naomi and Becky and Aggie.

INSPIRATIONAL

Inspirational romances to warm your heart & soul.

TITLES AVAILABLE NEXT MONTH

Available July 26, 2011

WYOMING SWEETHEARTS
The Granger Family Ranch
Jillian Hart

THE SHERIFF'S RUNAWAY BRIDE
Rocky Mountain Heirs
Arlene James

FAMILY BY DESIGN
Rosewood, Texas
Bonnie K. Winn

FIREMAN DAD
Betsy St. Amant

ONCE UPON A COWBOY
Pamela Tracy

AT HOME IN HIS HEART
Glynna Kaye

REQUEST YOUR FREE BOOKS!

2 FREE INSPIRATIONAL NOVELS
PLUS 2
FREE
MYSTERY GIFTS

YES! Please send me 2 FREE Love Inspired® novels and my 2 FREE mystery gifts (gifts are worth about $10). After receiving them, if I don't wish to receive any more books, I can return the shipping statement marked "cancel." If I don't cancel, I will receive 6 brand-new novels every month and be billed just $4.49 per book in the U.S. or $4.99 per book in Canada. That's a saving of at least 22% off the cover price. It's quite a bargain! Shipping and handling is just 50¢ per book in the U.S. and 75¢ per book in Canada.* I understand that accepting the 2 free books and gifts places me under no obligation to buy anything. I can always return a shipment and cancel at any time. Even if I never buy another book, the two free books and gifts are mine to keep forever. 105/305 IDN FEGR

Name _____ (PLEASE PRINT) _____

Address _____ Apt. # _____

City _____ State/Prov. _____ Zip/Postal Code _____

Signature (if under 18, a parent or guardian must sign) _____

Mail to the **Reader Service:**
IN U.S.A.: P.O. Box 1867, Buffalo, NY 14240-1867
IN CANADA: P.O. Box 609, Fort Erie, Ontario L2A 5X3

Not valid for current subscribers to Love Inspired books.

**Are you a subscriber to Love Inspired books
and want to receive the larger-print edition?
Call 1-800-873-8635 or visit www.ReaderService.com.**

* Terms and prices subject to change without notice. Prices do not include applicable taxes. Sales tax applicable in N.Y. Canadian residents will be charged applicable taxes. Offer not valid in Quebec. This offer is limited to one order per household. All orders subject to credit approval. Credit or debit balances in a customer's account(s) may be offset by any other outstanding balance owed by or to the customer. Please allow 4 to 6 weeks for delivery. Offer available while quantities last.

Your Privacy—The Reader Service is committed to protecting your privacy. Our Privacy Policy is available online at www.ReaderService.com or upon request from the Reader Service.

We make a portion of our mailing list available to reputable third parties that offer products we believe may interest you. If you prefer that we not exchange your name with third parties, or if you wish to clarify or modify your communication preferences, please visit us at www.ReaderService.com/consumerschoice or write to us at Reader Service Preference Service, P.O. Box 9062, Buffalo, NY 14269. Include your complete name and address.

LIREG11B

DEA Agent Paige Ashworth's new assignment is to work undercover at a local elementary school to find out how her partner and his girlfriend died while trying to take down a drug ring. Read on for a sneak preview of AGENT UNDERCOVER by Lynette Eason, available August 2011 only from Love Inspired Suspense.

Pain. That was Paige's first thought. Her first feeling. Her first piece of awareness.

It felt like shards of glass bit into her skull with relentless determination. Her eyes fluttered and she thought she saw someone seated in the chair next to her.

Why was she in bed?

Memories flitted back. Bits and pieces. A little boy. A school. A crosswalk. A speeding car.

And she'd pedaled like a madwoman to dart in front of the car to rescue the child.

A gasp escaped her and she woke a little more. The pain faded to a dull throb. Where was the little boy? Was he all right?

Warmth covered her left hand. Someone held it. Who?

Awareness struggled into full consciousness, and she opened her eyes to stare into one of the most beautiful faces she'd ever seen. Aquamarine eyes crinkled at the corners and full lips curved into a smile.

The lips spoke. "Hello, welcome back."

Another sweet face pushed its way into her line of sight. A little boy about six years old.

"Hi," she whispered.

The hand over hers squeezed. "You saved Will's life, you know."

She had? Will. The little boy had a name. "Oh. Good."

Her smiled slipped into a frown. "I was afraid I couldn't do
it. That car…"

"I'm Dylan Seabrook. This is my nephew, Will Price."

The name jolted her. Doing her best to keep her expression neutral, she simply smiled at him. She wanted to nod,
but didn't dare.

Closing her eyes, Paige could see the racing car coming
closer, hear the roar of the engine…

She flicked her eyelids up. "Did they catch him? Whoever was in the car?"

Dylan shook his head. "No. He—or she—never
stopped."

She sighed. "Well, I'm glad Will is okay. That's all that
really matters." Well, that, and whether or not she'd just
blown her cover to save this child—the son of the woman
whose death she was supposed to be investigating.

*For more, pick up AGENT UNDERCOVER
by Lynette Eason, available August 2011
from Love Inspired Suspense.*

Love Inspired

When Kylie Jones catches
her fiancé kissing another
girl moments before their
wedding, she runs—
smack into Deputy Sheriff
Zach Clayton! Zach is
very understanding to her
distress, but he's only in
town temporarily. Unless
Kylie can lead the love-
shy lawman to the wed-
ding they've *both* always
dreamed of…

The Sheriff's Runaway Bride
by Arlene James

ROCKY MOUNTAIN HEIRS

*Available August
wherever books are sold.*

www.LoveInspiredBooks.com

LI87686

Love Inspired HISTORICAL

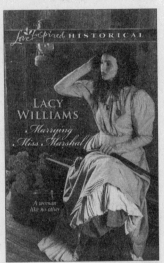

Fighting to earn respect as the new town marshal, Danna Carpenter teams up with detective Chas O'Grady for help. But when circumstances place them in a compromising situation, the town forces a more permanent partnership—marriage. If they can let down their guards with each other they might find that love is the greatest catch of all.

Marrying Miss Marshal
by
LACY WILLIAMS

Available August
wherever books are sold.

www.LoveInspiredBooks.com

LIH82881